Fool's
CAP
and Other Stories

Fool's
CAP
and Other Stories

KEITH WEAVER

IGUANA

Copyright @ 2019 Keith Weaver
Published by Iguana Books
720 Bathurst Street, Suite 303
Toronto, ON M5S 2R4

Publisher: Meghan Behse
Editor: Lee Parpart
Front cover image: courtesy of Shutterstock.com

ISBN 978-1-77180-384-7 (paperback)
ISBN 978-1-77180-385-4 (epub)
ISBN 978-1-77180-386-1 (Kindle)

This is an original print edition of *Fool's Cap.*

Contents

Crossing

I had just bought a bunch of those little plastic things you stick between your teeth when it happened.

At the last minute I remembered them — the little plastic things — and it just so happened that the Rexall on the corner was still open. It was 4:25 am. My eavesdropping stint had just finished.

I had come out of the Rexall, carrying my bag of toothpicks, when I heard tires screeching, then a smash, then a kind of thud. I peered around the corner. Saw a green Hyundai, one of those ugly-as-sin SUV/station wagon/sedan shapes, designed by computer and opinion survey. It seems that all car makers are moving toward the same general form. Not a car design at all, just a horrible mash-up of incompatible design ideas, and then they plane down the rough edges into revolting bulbous shapes.

The Hyundai sat there in the intersection, idling. About ten feet away, a form lay in the street. It looked like a person, and I was pretty sure he or she wasn't going to rise again. I heard a door slam. Must have been on the side of the car facing away from me. The tires screeched again, and the car took off down Jarvis Street.

On an early November morning at not yet four thirty, the sky was dark, despite a weak attempt by light to wash in from the east. In the buildings around me, there were no lights showing, and the tire noise caused none to be flicked on.

It was then that I saw her. She was at the corner, on the opposite side of the street from me, next to a crosswalk. About eight years old. Wide-eyed. Rigid. Petrified. Uncomprehending. I began crossing the street toward her, but her mouth opened as if she were about to scream, and then she bolted, ran into the park, crossed Wilton Street, and raced into a low-rise building. I knew the building. Community housing.

There was nothing else I could do, even though it was likely to cause me trouble later. I dragged out my cellphone and called the police and an ambulance. In less than a minute, a siren gave a short bleep at some traffic lights up Jarvis Street and to the west, just out of sight, and then a cruiser rounded the corner, all lights flashing. Less than another minute later, an ambulance rushed to the intersection, and pulled up not far from the victim, who still hadn't moved. By then the officer had made a call on his radio, climbed out of his cruiser, taken a half-dozen photographs of the scene, walked over to me, asked who I was and if I had seen the accident, told me to wait exactly where I was, and then began stringing yellow police tape to block off the intersection. As the paramedics attended to the victim, they exchanged looks with the policeman. One paramedic shook his head, and the policeman waved them to continue. They placed the victim on a stretcher, loaded him into the ambulance, and raced off. The nearest hospital was less than a minute away, and I guessed that either the poor bugger would be pulled back from the brink or declared dead there.

I turned and was face-to-face with the policeman, pen poised, and all business. His shadow beard told me that he was probably nearing the end of his shift. He was late thirties, powerfully built, not someone to cross, this impression confirmed by the bloodshot eyes, indicating that he was coming to the end of a hard night.

"Name?"

"Jackson Augustine."

"Address?"

I gave him my address, such as it is.

"What do you do?"

Here I decided on the minimalist approach. I do odd ends of work that match my skills and background. I'm a sort of private investigator, but never bothered to get my licence. Hate paperwork, you see. Waste of time. Plenty of people are prepared to pay me to do stuff. Mutual back-scratching, you understand. That's the story, anyway. But I really work for only one group, when you come right down to it.

"Handyman", I replied, economically.

"Handyman? What sort of handyman?"

"Anything anyone wants done."

"So, plumbing, carpentry…?"

"Yeah. That and some nightclub stuff."

"You do handyman work at nightclubs?"

"No. I help keep the peace."

"Bouncer? You're a little small for a bouncer."

"Size isn't everything." I didn't bother to mention my specialist training, or the fact that I hate violence, bullies, and, most of all, losing.

"What was the last club you worked?"

"Gerald's, on Richmond."

"And when I go down to Gerald's on Richmond, this will all check out?"

"Don't worry. It will."

He made quite a few notes before looking back up at me. I had to smile because as a sort of private investigator myself I know the drill: If you think someone might be up to something, you take your sweet time and make them wait. That way, the person you're pumping for information knows you're in charge.

"Okay. What did you see?"

"I was just coming out of the drug store, over there", I said, pointing toward the Rexall. "I bought these", and I held up the Rexall bag. "My receipt's right here. I didn't actually see the accident. I heard tires screech, then a crunching sound. Then a thud. I looked around the corner and saw a green Hyundai stopped just there, where the tire marks end. I heard a door slam, and the car screeched off that way, down Jarvis."

"You heard a door slam. Did you see the driver?"

"No. The windows were tinted, and the driver's side was facing away from me."

"The driver didn't get out?"

"I didn't see anyone do that. I assume he opened the door, looked at the person he had hit, slammed the door, and took off."

"Was anyone else in the car?"

"I don't know. As I said, the windows were tinted."

"You said *he* slammed the door. How do you know it was a man?"

"I don't. Figure of speech. I didn't see the driver at all."

The policeman made more notes.

"Did you see anyone else, anyone who might have seen what happened?"

"No."

"Anything else?"

"Yes. The licence number is CMTF 381."

"And you're just getting around to telling me that now?"

I said nothing in response.

The policeman made more notes.

"Okay. Give me a number where you can be reached. And can you come to the station with me now to fill out a statement?"

This didn't sound like a request.

"Sure."

By then, another police vehicle had arrived. Two men got out and spoke briefly to my policeman, then began making measurements.

My policeman, whose name, I discovered, was Fountain, drove me to the station. I filled out a report, signed it, and was back outside by eight o'clock. I went home and crashed, having spent all night working. I awoke just after noon, showered, shaved, and headed off to the Jason George for what would turn out to be my only meal of the day.

There was the usual crowd, and the place was doing a good business. I chose a table for two, ordered steak and eggs and a large glass of water, and then surveyed the room. Ronnie, who made a good living on shady real estate deals, was there. Howard was there. He was recently retired as a fireman — a taciturn but very pleasant fellow who does a lot of volunteering in the community. Then there was Jinksie. Jinksie Navarro is one of the most informed people I know, but he's called Jinksie for a reason. Pretty much anything he gets involved in as an active participant goes south very quickly. And when I say south, I mean having no hope of retrieval.

Jinksie smiled and waved, and to my despair, he rose, picked up his beer, which looked as though he hadn't even taken a sip of it, and started toward my table.

"Hi Jinksie. How are things?"

"Good Jacky. You?"

"Okay."

"Hear about the accident down on Jarvis this morning?"

"Didn't need to. I saw it."

Jinksie's face went into 'eager tell me all' mode, but just then my meal arrived, and I wasted no time starting on it, giving me a good reason to ignore all the questions I expected him to direct at me.

I was surprised when Jinksie didn't immediately start trying to pump me. Instead, he sipped his beer and smiled at me again.

"And did you hear about Willie Anderson?"

Willie Anderson is a small time crook-for-hire who never wants to get involved in anything messy, so he never gets paid much. He also likes the ponies, and poker, but he's no good at either of them, so he's very often in someone's bad books.

"No. What's up with Willie?"

"He's dead. Found this morning in his crummy little flat. Bullet to the back of the head."

Now this was news. There was a story making the rounds that Willie had really pissed off Jonathan Halpern. If it was Jonathan who had finally taken Willie off the board, then Willie must have screwed up something fearsome.

"When did they find him, Jinksie?"

"About nine o'clock, I hear."

"Do you know who did it? Why? When?"

"Don't know who or why. But the word is that he was done in between about three and five o'clock this morning."

How Jinksie gets this information, I do not know. But the weird thing is that he's rarely wrong. So if he says something, it's a good idea not to dismiss it too quickly.

"Any idea who did it?"

"No. None. And it doesn't seem to make a lot of sense. If a guy owes you money, knocking him off isn't a bright idea. And it's pretty obvious that it wasn't a bit of roughing up that got out of hand."

I was getting an uncomfortable feeling.

"Do you have any info on what else Willie might have been involved in, Jinksie? Something more heavy weight?"

"You're just full of questions, Jacky. Has this got you worried?"

"No. Not at all. But you know how important information is, Jinksie. I'm just a small-time guy too. Maybe I should be keeping a closer eye on my own back."

Jinksie chuckled.

"You're not a crook, Jacky. You just work in a grey area."

"True. But Willie being erased is an event, something that might be full of information. And the thing about information is that it can be true, false, or nothing, depending on how you read it."

"What are you saying, Jacky?"

It seemed that Jinksie's antenna had gone into a high amplitude twitch.

"I'm just saying that this Willie thing doesn't make sense to me. And that might mean I'm missing something."

"Like what?"

"Well, if I knew that, Jinksie, we wouldn't be having this chat, would we?"

We sat in silence for a few minutes while it looked like I was sipping my water and reflecting on the state of the cosmos. What I really was doing was considering some possibilities. Willie must have got in the way of something important. He knew something, or he saw something, or he did something, that he shouldn't have known, seen, or done.

I set down my water glass and smiled at Jinksie.

"Another one, Jinksie?"

"You buying?"

"Sure. Why not? You've been generous with your information."

I waved toward the bar. The man at the till held up two fingers and mouthed 'Two more?', and I nodded. Jinksie's second pint and my second water arrived in what seemed like record time.

We saluted each other with our glasses and drank. Then I tried again on an earlier question.

"So Jinksie, you were a bit cagey a minute ago on what else Willie might have been involved in. What do you know about his activities lately?"

"Just the usual. Small stuff ... mostly."

"Mostly? What does 'mostly' mean?"

Jinksie hesitated here. But then he looked up and eyed me closely.

"How much information do you think a pint buys you, Jacky?"

I waved at him impatiently.

"Come on Jinksie. So I'll owe you a favour. When something like this happens to a small-time guy like Willie, it's wise for everyone in the same category to sit up and take note. I just want to have a better idea what I should be taking note of. And it seems to me that you're in that category too."

"I had a chat with Willie a few days ago", Jinksie said, after a long pause. "He was upbeat. Looked confident. He said he'd turned a corner."

Jinksie stopped and began looking like he needed a prod.

"You aren't nodding off, are you Jinksie? What came next?"

"Not much, Jacky. It was odd. Willie just seemed different."

"Sounds like he had a new number lined up", I said.

"That's what I thought too."

"But…?" I added when it began looking like Jinksie had stalled again.

"No. No but. I just didn't get anything more out of him. But it did seem almost that I would be talking to him again soon, and that the next time we met the big score would be behind him."

"Drugs?" I asked.

"Probably. It's one way to make a lot of money fast. But there's no unclaimed turf in the drugs game. Anybody new is bound to find themselves in someone's crosshairs."

"Halpern?"

"Seems likely."

We finished our drinks, talked about other things for a while, then I said I had to go off and look after business. The uncomfortable feeling I had earlier had now gained some weight.

It took only about half an hour of asking around to find the little girl. I spent another forty minutes making the arrangements that I suspected would be needed later. When I knocked on the door of her apartment, it seemed at first that nobody was home, but eventually the door opened a crack.

"What do you want?"

The question came from a face that looked raddled by misfortune, worry, and booze. Her blue eyes, which once must have been attractive, even alluring, were faded and bloodshot. Strings of unwashed blond hair hung down past cheeks whose skin had an unhealthy pallor.

"Mrs. Warren?" I asked in as kindly a voice as possible.

"Who are you? What do you want?"

"I'd like to speak to you. My name is Jackson Augustine. I'm not from the police or any of the social services, and I'm not a reporter. It's about the accident this morning out on Jarvis Street."

"What about it?"

"I was a witness to it. So was your daughter. I saw her there. The police asked me if I saw anybody else who might have seen the accident, and I said no. Please. I'm asking just for five minutes."

"There's no reason I should talk to you. Go away."

She began trying to close the door, but I already had one sturdy boot next to the door frame, and the door wouldn't move.

"There *is* a reason you should speak to me, Mrs. Warren. There are a lot of buildings around here that have views of that intersection. It's quite possible that somebody else might have seen the accident, and might have seen your daughter there as well. If so, the police will find out eventually, and then they will come here and you won't be able to tell them to go away."

She hesitated.

"Please. Just five minutes."

There was the sound of the safety chain being withdrawn, the door then opened, and she made a hesitant and half-hearted gesture inviting me in. The place was the most depressing scene of confused untidiness, but I advanced toward the only uncluttered chair. The young girl I had seen early that morning was standing wide-eyed behind a sofa.

"You need a reason to trust me", I said. "Do you know Ahmed down at the convenience store on the corner?"

"Yes, but..."

"Please phone him. Here's his number", I said, and passed her one of Ahmed's cards. She hesitated.

"Please. Ask Ahmed if he knows me and if I can be trusted. But don't let him know that I'm here."

She moved to her phone and made the call. She asked Ahmed about me. I could hear his happy laugh from where I sat.

"I want him to do some work for me. Can I trust him?"

The happy laugh rolled across the room once more. They had a brief exchange.

"Okay. Thanks Ahmed."

I offered them both a faint smile, then took the initiative.

"I think the accident this morning really was an accident. But something else happened near here last night, and I want to know whether that and the accident were linked."

"How would I...?" Mrs. Warren began, but I raised a hand indicating that I would try to explain.

"Sometime early this morning, there was a murder about three blocks from here. The man driving the car involved in that accident down there also might have been involved in the other event. I want to find out whether that's the case."

"How does that involve me?"

"Your daughter saw him at the accident. It's almost certain he saw her there. If he was involved in the murder, then he will know that she might be able to identify him."

"She won't. We'll just tell the police..."

"It's not a matter of telling the police, I'm afraid. If he thinks she could identify him, he might try to do something to prevent that."

"What could he ...? Oh no! Oh my God no!"

She moved behind the sofa and put a protective arm over her daughter's shoulder.

"What's all this to you?" she said, her suspicions suddenly in high gear once again.

"I just want to help", I said. "God knows I've done little enough in the past to help other people, but in this case I think I can do something and I want to do something."

"What can you do?" she asked.

I explained what I had in mind. She appeared unconvinced, and her expression told me that everyone else she had trusted in the past had crapped out on her. But finally she gave a reluctant agreement.

"This man wants to ask you some questions, Sarah", she said in a tone that really struck a chord with me. It was so full of love.

I remained where I was, looked at the girl, and smiled.

"Sarah. You were there this morning, down at the intersection, and you saw me. Do you remember that?"

She looked at her mother, who squeezed her shoulder. Sarah looked at me, then nodded.

"And I started across the street toward you. But I'm afraid I scared you, and I'm sorry about that. I didn't mean to scare you."

I waited a moment, making sure that what I said had registered.

"Now Sarah. This is important. Did you see the man who was driving the car?"

Another shoulder squeeze from her mother.

Another nod from Sarah.

"What did he look like? For example, what colour was his hair?"

There was a long delay here. Sarah looked at her mother, her expression signalling the wish that all this would just go away.

A smile from her mother and two more shoulder squeezes.

"Ye ... yellow."

"And did he have something on his face? Just here?" I asked, drawing a finger down my left cheek.

The answer came out after another delay.

"Purple."

I gave Sarah a big smile.

"Can I speak to you?" I said to Mrs. Warren.

She nodded, and asked Sarah to go and get ready for her nap.

We sat facing each other in that untidy room, one that was filled by the detritus of a life, by the presence of a woman in the grip of alcohol and the many aspects of poverty, but a room also warmed by a strong bond between the woman and her daughter, possibly the only thing of value they both possessed.

"A blond-haired man", I said, "who has a large scar on his left cheek. He goes by the name of Sidney, and he's involved in a drug racket. I suspect that he was responsible for the murder early this morning and that it was just his bad luck to be involved in that accident."

We talked for another minute.

"So it is what you thought?" she asked.

"It looks that way."

"What will happen now?"

"Well, the police will probably have the same suspicion I had…"

"So. They'll arrest this man? And that will be the end of it?"

I'm sure she hoped that fervently but didn't believe it.

"They will likely detain him and ask him a lot of questions. But I also expect that he will have answers. No, I doubt that they'll be able to hold him."

"So… What can I do?" Her face showed mixed emotions: great concern for her daughter, determination to protect her, and fear born of deep love. But her compulsive hand motions revealed something else — helplessness.

I explained what I had in mind, that she and her daughter needed to get away, and I told her about a friend's place. I told her how nice and peaceful it was, and I explained how I proposed to get them there.

"…and when you get to Frederick Street, a Beck taxi will pull up at the curb, the driver will get out and open the back doors, and you and your daughter will get in."

"And then?"

"And then you'll be driven a short distance to where I'll meet you, and we'll go the rest of the way from there. You should pack enough for about a week."

"Right now?"

"Yes."

"When do we do this?"

"This afternoon."

"This afternoon? Is there such a rush?"

"I don't know. But I think you shouldn't be waiting to find out."

She went off to pack.

I made a quick phone call. All I said was, "Get ready."

Twenty minutes later, she reappeared, carrying a battered brown suitcase, which she placed by the door. She had also obviously washed her face, put on some light makeup, combed her hair, and changed into a clean pair of jeans and a grey blouse. My face must have telegraphed that she was now easy to look at, because she failed to suppress a little smile of pleasure.

"Good", I said. "I'll be back in about ten minutes, so at quarter to four. We can go downstairs together, but you leave the building first."

"What about you?"

"I'll follow just a few minutes later."

Seeing her look of concern, I said, "It's okay. Please trust me. I'll be right back. When I return, I'll knock three times, then two times, then one time." She nodded.

Then I left, walked down one floor, and made three telephone calls, double-checking all the arrangements I had made earlier.

The door to Mrs. Warren's apartment opened immediately when I knocked. I entered.

"All ready?" I asked.

"Yes", she said, and went across the room to fuss touchingly with her daughter's hair, the collar of her slightly shabby dress. I set my tablet down on top of a small bookcase. "Let me carry your case down", I said. She looked around and nodded, I picked up the case, we left the apartment, she locked up, and we started down the stairs.

"Oh! Damn!" I said, when we were halfway down the second flight of steps. "I've left my tablet in your apartment. If you give me your keys, I'll just go and get it." I hurried back upstairs, keys in hand, did what needed to be done, picked up the tablet, and joined them a few minutes later.

We carried on down the stairs. When we reached the front door, I set down her case on its wheels. "You can take it from here. Just walk along to Frederick Street, and when the Beck taxi pulls up, climb in. I'll see you again in a few minutes."

She was the picture of uncertainty, but they went out the door, onto the street, turned right, and were soon out of my field of vision. The day was failing. The light was already dim. Streetlights had switched themselves on. I walked out the door about thirty seconds later, saw that they were now a good distance down the block, and turned to the left. A grey Pontiac was sitting by the curb. I walked up to it, opened the front passenger door, and got in.

"Hi Jacky."

"Hi Wilf. How are things?"

"Good. Looks like nobody is following them. Where to?"

"They're going to the car park at the Loblaws, Leslie and Lakeshore. Just follow them at a distance."

"Okay Jacky."

I saw them get into the Beck taxi. It pulled away, and Wilf started after them. Ten minutes later, we entered the Loblaws car park. The taxi was parked close to the Loblaws entrance and exit. Wilf had pulled into a spot further back, next to another grey Pontiac.

Then we waited. Five minutes. Ten minutes.

"Okay", I said to Wilf. "I think we're good. You know where we're going next?"

"Yes."

"Okay. Let's swap now. You just follow me and we'll make the switch."

He nodded.

Wilf climbed out of the car, walked to the taxi, and soon was coming back with Mrs. Warren, Sarah, and their case. The taxi pulled away. I had emerged from the car, and took the suitcase and said a few words to Mrs. Warren. Then she, Sarah, and Wilf got back into the grey Pontiac he had just left. I looked around and soon found what I wanted. It wasn't perfect, but it would have to do. It was an articulated truck parked at one side of the large Loblaws store. I threw the suitcase into the trunk of the second grey Pontiac, climbed in behind the wheel, started it, and drove around behind the articulated truck. Wilf followed in the first grey Pontiac, and both cars were now behind the truck, out of sight from three sides. I jumped out of my car, ran to the first Pontiac, and hustled the woman and the girl back to my car.

"Lie down on the back seat, completely out of sight! Quickly!"

When they were in and it all looked good, I jumped back in the car, left the Loblaws car park, turned south on Leslie, and then east on Lakeshore.

"Where are we going?" Mrs. Warren said. She sounded frightened.

"Right away, we're going to Oshawa. Then we'll be heading for Huntsville. Please try not to be alarmed. I know all this seems very strange, but everything we're doing is for a good reason. Please make yourself as comfortable as you can. Everything will be alright soon."

I could hear her whispering to Sarah, but that stopped after a few minutes, and I drove on in silence. It took almost an hour and a half to reach Oshawa, and I drove to another large, busy supermarket near the centre of town. I drove around a bit in the car park, as though looking for a spot, then parked facing the entrance at the east side of the car park. About ten minutes later, I gave a quick flash of the car's headlights. Wilf pulled into the parking spot immediately to my left.

"My friend Wilf is going to drive this car for the next half hour. I'll follow right behind in another car. From there, I'll be driving the rest of the way. Don't worry. We'll soon be where we're going. Okay?"

There was a hesitant 'Okay' from Mrs. Warren.

Wilf and I switched cars.

"You know where to go next, Wilf", I said through his open window. He nodded.

Wilf left the shopping centre car park first. I followed ten minutes later. In about forty-five minutes we were once again parked side by side in central Port Perry. Wilf and I both got out of our cars. It was now dark.

"Thanks Wilf. I'll settle with you when we're back in town."

"No problem", he said, giving me a friendly tap on the shoulder. Then he climbed into the car I had just left, and drove off. I got into the car Wilf had vacated.

"Okay. We're on the way now, the final leg", I said to my backseat passengers.

"How long?" Mrs. Warren asked.

"About two and a half hours. Are you reasonably comfortable?"

"No. But we'll manage." She sounded resigned and still none too happy, but at least not afraid.

It was about two hours and forty minutes later when we pulled into the drive of a large cottage off Brunel Road just outside Huntsville. I brought the car as close to the front door as I could, got out, and opened both back doors.

"We're here, at last, and I'm sorry for what must have been an uncomfortable ride. Here, let me help you both."

They climbed unsteadily out of the car and looked around while I lifted the suitcase out of the trunk. It was now well after eight o'clock and had been fully dark for some time, so there wasn't much to see. But there were lights on in the house and a porch light came on as we were standing there.

"Jacky? Is that you?"

"Stan. Yes, it's me."

"Do you need any help?"

"No. Thanks Stan. We're fine."

Mrs. Warren cast me a questioning look. It was likely that she was disoriented, and I suspected that she was worrying about being hopelessly outclassed socially.

"Don't worry", I said to her quietly. "Stan is one of us."

We all trooped inside, Stan explained the living arrangements: guests on the lower level, Sylvia and Stan on the upper level, house built into the side of a hill.

"How is Sylvia?" I asked.

"Fine. Long day. Been painting all day. Made an early night of it."

"I'll take them downstairs, Stan, if that's alright with you."

"Fine, yes. Now that you're here, I think I'll turn in as well. So I'll see you in the morning." He smiled at Sarah and Mrs. Warren and moved off down the hall.

It took no time for them to find their feet on their lower-level accommodation, and they both looked around at what must have seemed to them like opulent surroundings. Sarah was clearly tired, but she smiled at the possibility of a shower. I showed them where the bathroom was, and Mrs. Warren led Sarah off, saying as she went that she would bring what Sarah needed to the bathroom. The lower level consisted of a generous bedroom with an ensuite bathroom, a large sitting room, which had sliding doors onto an outdoor patio, and a swing door into a well-equipped kitchen. Mrs. Warren returned from the bathroom, opened the suitcase, removed what were evidently some of Sarah's clothes and a nightdress, and took them to the bathroom. When she returned, we settled into chairs in the sitting room.

"What's this all about?" she asked, phrasing it as a plea, a request for information, and not as a challenge.

"I know that this is an unusual situation, but there's nothing to be concerned about. I'm in a position to help, and that's what I'm doing."

"I'm poor, Mr. Augustine, and I'm grateful for your help, but this" — she waved at the room we were in — "this makes me uncomfortable. I'd like an explanation. It doesn't need to be right now, but..."

I said to Mrs. Warren that this would be their home for at least the next few days, until it became clear how the situation back in Toronto would develop. Riding roughshod over her rising objection, I explained that she had been caught, innocently, in the middle of something potentially very dangerous, and that fleeing in a manner unknown to anyone except us, to a place and to people to whom she had had no previous connection whatever, was the best, quickest, and easiest way to get out of that bad situation.

"But what...? How...?"

"You just need to trust me. The less you know, the better."

I deliberately held her gaze slightly too long. She nodded agreement, and looked away.

"I'm going back to Toronto tonight, and —"

"Tonight?" Her alarm at being left alone rose like a sea monster.

"Don't worry. I'll be in very regular contact, through Stan. There's no telephone on this level of the house. Please don't try to contact anybody. I mean nobody. If you need to speak to me, ask Stan. Stan and Sylvia are both delightful people. I've known them both for more than twenty years. They know you're in a difficult situation, but nothing more. Please just try to treat this as a break, a sort of holiday. While you're here, nothing can happen to you."

She wasn't at all happy, but her expression said that she was accepting something that appeared to be unavoidable.

"One more thing", I said. "May I have the keys to your apartment? Nothing sinister here. But if you find you need anything from it, I can get it for you."

She handed over the keys. I spent more time reassuring her, said once again that I would be in touch, and then left. On the way back, I had a fairly long cellphone conversation with Jinksie. I made it back to Toronto just after midnight, hoping that I hadn't missed anything.

I made my way to Mrs. Warren's small apartment and let myself in. The place was dark, and I had time to set up the camera in the bedroom. I moved one of the kitchen chairs into the bathroom, checked that the bathroom door didn't squeak, then closed it to just a couple of inches short of being fully shut. After that I took off my shoes, sat down on the chair, and waited.

I began to wonder whether I had judged things correctly, but then the noise I expected began at about two thirty. It was the sound of somebody picking a door lock. A few moments later, a shade passed by the bathroom door. I heard the door to the bedroom open. I crept from the bathroom toward the bedroom door. There was movement inside. Violent movement.

"It's over, Sidney", I said loudly, at the same time flicking on the light.

Sidney swung around, ready to attack, until he saw the weapon in my hand. He was still holding the long hunting knife. There were holes, tears, in the bedclothes covering the forms on the two beds.

Sidney looked down. There was no blood on the knife. Anger flooded his face as he realized he had been played, and without thinking he charged, the knife raised over his head. This came to a stop quickly when my .38 cracked hard against his elbow, then across the side of his head. He fell to the floor. Taking the knife from him, I cut off the lamp cord, and tied his hands behind his back.

Walking into the main room of Mrs. Warren's small apartment, I pulled out my cellphone and placed a call to a shady policeman. A groggy voice mumbled something after the sixth ring. He wasn't pleased.

"What? Right now? In the middle of the night?"

"Yeah. Right now, very important. Try to get here five minutes ago."

I gave him the address, then hung up.

I placed another call immediately to Jinksie, who picked up after the fifth ring.

"Shit Jacky! Do you know what time it is?"

"Just listen, Jinksie", and I explained the situation to him.

"Holy shit! What are you going to do, Jacky?"

"Good night Jinksie", I said, then hung up. My phone rang three times in the next ten minutes. Jinksie. I ignored it.

A large pitcher of water thrown over Sidney's head brought him round fairly quickly.

"Come on Sidney. On your feet."

He looked at the beds, the forms in them, pillows and blankets I had arranged when I returned at about four o'clock the previous afternoon, nominally to retrieve my tablet.

"What...?"

"They're not here, Sidney", I said.

"Who's not here?" he responded, having recouped some of his wits. "I don't know what you're talking about."

"Stop wasting time, Sidney. You were sent here to kill that little girl and her mother. The tape will show you trying to do exactly that, and you'll need to explain those images", I said, pointing to the small camera on top of the bookcase. "Besides, someone else is coming here to have a quiet chat with you."

There was real fear in his eyes now.

"No. It's not Halpern."

He just looked at me sullenly.

"It's Cal Dalton", I said. It was clear that Sidney knew what that meant.

"I really had no choice", Sidney said after a long delay. "Halpern gave me no choice." A short delay. "If only there hadn't been that accident..."

"So Halpern told you to clean up the loose ends, is that it?"

Sidney nodded. "Yes, that would have been the end of it."

"And everything would have gone back to normal then, right?"

"Right."

"Wrong, Sidney. Then you would have been the loose end. And guess what?"

In the end, things worked out after a fashion. Dalton arrived about ten minutes later, at which point I left. I expect that Dalton pumped Sidney dry, then took him away.

The information I had given to Jinksie was dynamite, and it blew the lids off a couple of drug empires. Within a day, the operations run by Halpern and Cheng were in ruins. Five bodies were found in various places. Cheng was dead. Halpern was seriously wounded and taken into custody. Sidney had decided to sing.

The higher-ups in the police weren't happy outwardly, because the politicians were outraged at the violence and wanted answers. 'Drug war that broke out spontaneously, none of it foreseen' was the best answer they ever got.

I had had enough. I told my minder that I was finished with undercover work, and finished with the police. Time to wash away the unspeakably bad taste and move on.

Leslie and Sarah Warren moved back to their place about two weeks after they had left. I helped them sort things out. I had a chat with Ahmed, told him that quiet arrangements with people like Mrs. Warren could get him into serious trouble. Had another quiet chat with Leslie Warren, telling her that there should be no repeats of sending Sarah out in the middle of the night to pick up cigarettes in a brown paper bag from Ahmed. This became unimportant when she decided to give up smoking. I helped her find a job at Metro. Howard agreed to meet Sarah from school and walk her home.

Weeks later, over a glass of wine, Leslie asked me, in a roundabout way, whether we had a future.

"We all have futures", I said.

I smiled at her...

Oh Deer!

It was a beautiful house in an ideal setting. I fell in love with the spot the first time I saw it and had to hold down pangs of jealousy that threatened to escape, complete with juvenile barbs. This was a place where I belonged, and Jacob had beaten me to it!

The approach is what catches one's attention first: a storybook drive, winding past trees that know their own stately elegance. This drive opens onto a flat clearing whose edges are defined by dense growths of conifer, in the middle of which sits the house.

The house.

It is a modern log construction, nineteenth century in appearance, but with twenty-first century specifications. The morticed cedar logs needed no caulking; they were generously covered by durable sealant, and supplemented by high R-factor insulation that was sandwiched between the log exterior and the tongue and groove interior panelling. Long-life cast iron roofing that is a dead ringer for terracotta tile completes the picture.

"Fantastic, Jacob! How did you find this place? And where did you get the house design?"

The lot had been identified at the end of a dogged three-month search, while the house design turned out to be a local inspiration that Jacob had taken a lot of effort modifying. I was impressed by one thing after another.

There was the visual impact on first approach, a natural integration that soon yielded to the unconscious triage separating house from carefully placed trees and shrubs, patches of flower garden, and strategically placed bird feeders. These feeders, once one had spotted them, drew the eye immediately; each one was different in design and decorative motif, and they were all placed to maximize human enjoyment and avian privacy. Then there was the car port, which had been thoughtfully sequestered in a space screened from view by further clumps of conifers. Even the picnic table and loungers had been carefully placed on the southern and most private side of the house, in a natural suntrap. Every detail of the property had been thought through, and I couldn't stop smiling as Jacob led me from one feature to the next.

"And then", he said, waving me to his left, "we have…"

I was clearly being led toward something important, but I was moving more slowly. Whereas Jacob was familiar with every detail of the property, this was my first visit, and there was a lot to take in. I needed time just to look and to absorb all the details of the surroundings.

Jacob had stopped about fifty feet from the vegetable garden, and from that spot, the care he had taken in deciding everything about his property became evident. There was, first of all, the property's general location. In the distance, about three or four kilometres away, the Atlantic appeared to be dozing fitfully. Of the many islands I knew were out there, three were visible through the haze. It was one of those perfect Nova Scotia days: sunny, warm, but not brassy or overwhelming. Waves of evergreens seemed to wash up toward us from the Atlantic. The ruggedness and self-reliance of everything around me was evident: the grass that had been coaxed to clothe, barely, a rocky, undulating substrate endowed with only a thin soil cover; the unselfconsciousness of the trees, which appeared to huddle against wind and weather; and the relative flamboyance of the native shrubs — witch hazel, red-osier dogwood, pin cherry, and northern bayberry.

The exception to all this, and the thing that drew my attention next, was the vegetable garden.

The soil looked rich and dark, a contrast to the thin, greyish-brown rocky soil elsewhere on the property. Evidently the hand of a devoted gardener had showered humus and TLC onto this favoured plot, giving it a radiant botanic tilth.

But there was the fence. Jacob hastened to explain.

"It's because of the deer. I have nothing against them, but they can crop an entire grown garden right down to the soil in a single night."

I looked up toward the top of the nine-foot high fence.

"And they can jump. Like you wouldn't believe."

We talked about this a bit more, and on his cellphone Jacob showed me pictures of deer — dainty, elegant, beautiful creatures, seemingly without fear, and anathema to his garden.

We continued our slow stroll. To do justice to the entire three acres took time, and we talked about our common past in central Canada, Jacob's decision to retire early, and the fervent desire of his wife, Pamela, to move Down East, to Nova Scotia, where Jacob had his roots. He described their long search fondly. First it was Sackville. Then they looked at Truro, Wolfeville, and Windsor. Then Mahone Bay. Finally they settled on Standish, not far from Lunenburg.

"It was tough. Pamela liked all the places, and we wavered among them for quite a long time. No, it didn't matter", Jacob said, noticing my quizzical expression. "The search itself was very enjoyable. And we had no particular deadline."

"Was it this property...?"

"Yep. As soon as Pamela saw this place, even though there was no house on it, that was the end of the search."

I had always known that Jacob was something of an amateur botanist, but his knowledge of the trees on his property, as well as the shrubs, the wildflowers, and even the different grasses, left me feeling inadequate. We crossed the neat gravel path just as it emerged from what he referred to as his arboreal gates, and headed, still at a strolling pace, toward a dip in the land near the southern edge of his property. In this area the ground became, by turns, rough and then spongy, so the grass grew luxuriantly, unclipped. The slope we were descending met another, similar, slope falling down more steeply from the opposite direction, and together they formed a sort of woodland cleavage, which retreated demurely into a patchy V-neck garment of ferns, conifer saplings, and struggling chokecherries. Close to the point where the foliage obscured all view, there was a clump of purplish plants.

"Aren't those pitcher plants?" I asked.

"They are", Jacob said. "And judging by their health, there must be quite a few fairly dopey insects down there."

We returned toward the house, walked all around it, strolled out through the arboreal gates, and then returned to the picnic table and two large, welcoming bottles of Propeller. We clinked the necks of the bottles, and glugged, heads back, eyes closed, and faces toward the sun.

The first half of my bottle of Propeller disappeared alarmingly fast, but Jacob waved to the cooler sitting next to the wall of the house. No need to tolerate any 'half empty' anxiety here.

All around us the birds were exclaiming forcefully, saying whatever they say to declare that the sun is shining and life is good. My gaze wandered again to the garden, and inevitably to the fence and its cocky air of intrusion.

Jacob followed my gaze.

"Anything lower than six feet just isn't high enough. Nine feet is beyond the ability of even the best of them. But you're right", and he scowled at the fence. "If I could think of another way, I would do it."

A short silence followed, which Jacob himself interrupted.

"In case you might be about to suggest it, I'm not going to shoot them. They're just trying to survive. Besides, any hunting should be strictly for the pot, a need that arises rarely if at all these days, and every hunter ought to be skilled enough to make a clean kill every time. These stories of wounded animals limping into the forest to die in pain hours or days later is enough to demand a blanket ban on hunting."

"I wasn't about to make any suggestion like that", I said. "But I remember my sister's experience working as a secretary in northern Ontario. The people there would gladly trade venison or moose for beef. Hard for them to get beef, and expensive even when it was available."

We stood looking at the fence for a time.

"What are their natural enemies, the deer, I mean?" I asked.

"Humans, coyotes, and bobcats or lynx, but it's not as though the deer population is out of control in the province."

"Are there coyotes around here?"

"I'm sure there are. But I've never seen one. And I've never come across a deer carcass. And as long as there are plenty of hares around, the pressure on the deer population is moderate."

"What about around here? I mean as opposed to a provincial average?"

"I don't have any numbers. But it's not unusual to see deer in this area. To some extent they seem to have adjusted to people, and they probably recognize that even in fairly low population density areas like this, having hunters around is rare."

"Have you seen deer here then?"

"Oh yes. Fairly often, if I'm up early and don't make any noise, I can see one or two of them out on the grass, or looking through the fence around the garden."

"But they move away as soon as you come outside?"

"Yes. Immediately. But out of caution, it seems, not in a panic."

The sky had cleared. The Atlantic glinted in the distance. The suntrap next to Jacob's house was doing its work, and we both reached for another Propeller. I closed my eyes. Today, life was easy. I listened to the sounds around us, a muted cacophony of birdsong and buzzing insects. I drifted, thinking of nothing and everything. There was the warmth of the sun, and a general warm feeling that came from somewhere else...

I don't know why, but the mad idea occurred to me just as I was opening my bottle. The cap made an unexpectedly loud pop. I described my idea briefly to Jacob.

"Another natural predator?" he exclaimed, his eyebrows practically vanishing into his hairline. "What sort of predator?"

I explained what I had in mind. I expected him to scoff, throw cold water over the whole thing, tell me I was nuts. He didn't. We talked about it for a few minutes. Then Jacob went back to the house and returned with a pad of paper and two pens. We then spent what seemed to be quite a long time working out possibilities, details.

"We could get an NSERC grant", I suggested. Jacob's expression was more than doubtful.

"You still have connections at the university, at Dalhousie, don't you?" I asked.

"Yes, but … this!"

"Nothing ventured", I said, and cast Jacob what I hoped was a challenging look.

Well, the short version is that we agreed to give it a try. At best it would be interesting. At worst it would be a short-lived lark. I promised to take the lead. We spent another hour sketching out a rough plan, had another Propeller each, then shelved the whole thing. I remember looking out again to the Atlantic, having lost track of time.

That evening we had a delightful meal at Jacob's picnic table. Pamela, Jacob, and I had prepared the meal together. A light breeze was wafting toward us from the Atlantic, as the trees around us swayed in a delicate communal dance. We didn't need to say anything; there was nothing to be said. Then, after a ten-minute silence while we enjoyed the glow from our meals and the wine, a delicate young doe stepped carefully from the evergreens, looked around cautiously, then quietly withdrew.

"Beautiful", I said, almost involuntarily.

"Yes. If only they would leave my garden alone."

The next three days passed as though in a dream. Time seemed alternately to stretch and contract. Images of the Fisheries Museum of the Atlantic, Blue Rocks, the Hank Snow Home Town Museum, Brier Island, the Saltbox Brewery, and the many other places I'd visited swam before me, along with mental pictures of deer, fences, and masses of waving chlorophyll. It was magical. And always there was the return to Pamela and Jacob's delightful home.

All too soon, it was over. I was back at Stanfield Airport saying goodbye to Jacob, and then Nova Scotia dropped down and drifted away to the east.

Back in Toronto, time seemed to continue flowing through a dreamscape. Against my every expectation, our NSERC grant application was accepted, at the full funding requested. Jacob and I began work immediately. We could do a lot independently, me in Toronto and Jacob in Nova Scotia, but soon the need for work on the ground became unavoidable. There were many trips for me to Lunenburg.

At some point, the project just seemed to take off, unexpectedly, irrationally, wildly. Time became compressed, and space was contorted.

Within just three months, we had our first success. We had produced a pitcher plant that was three feet tall and had an opening almost a foot in diameter. We pushed ahead as quickly as possible. My visits to Lunenburg became more frequent, and while I was there our days were long.

Five months after our project was initiated, we had generated a pitcher plant that was six feet tall and had an opening two and a half feet in diameter.

The first sign of trouble came just a few days later. We were awakened early one morning by a series of pitiful and panicked yelping cries. I pulled on trousers and headed downstairs. Before I could reach the back door to Jacob's house, the cries had ceased. As I moved outside, I could hear Jacob stumbling down the stairs, and Pamela upstairs asking anxiously what was wrong.

I headed toward our research site next to the garden. What I saw chilled me. The pitcher plant had changed during the night. It now had a bowl that lay sideways along the grass, was ten feet long, and four and a half feet in diameter, and as I approached it, I knew what the commotion had been about. Inside the bowl was the inert body of a spaniel, and the plant had already begun to dissolve it. I drew back in horror, and just as Jacob approached, a gurgle caused us both to leap away.

The plant had belched.

There was nothing we could do for the dog, so we went back inside to have a quick breakfast and decide what our next step should be. The toast and coffee had a very odd taste, but we downed it and then went back outside. There we found that in just that short time events had taken a much darker turn.

The pitcher plant was no longer there.

Looking around, I suddenly had a very cold feeling in the pit of my stomach. Strewn across the grass, past Jacob's house, was a trail of bones.

The dog's bones.

The plant had become mobile. It was now out there, somewhere, wandering freely.

Frankenpitcher.

The word rose up before me like something out of a Poe story.

The plant was indeed now large enough to take a deer. We had met our objective. But it was also at liberty. It could easily swallow other dogs, cats, racoons...

Oh! My God!

Children!

It would be able to swallow a child!

The morning sun glared at me accusingly.

The trees wobbled and swam as though in a hall of mirrors. Colours around me were now garish. Plasticine porters and marmalade skies had nothing on this!

Telephone! I needed to alert the authorities. But, oh shit! Would they believe me?

My legs were rubber as I tried to return to Jacob's kitchen. The telephone was stuck to the wall. I couldn't lift it off its rest. A cellphone was lying on the counter; I scooped it up, but it slumped to a sort of liquid the consistency of thick gravy and dripped to the floor.

I collapsed into a chair, panicked but benumbed at the same time. Light was flooding from everywhere it seemed. Everything was confusion. But I had to make another attempt.

Had to make...

Another...

I began to shake. Just what I need, I thought, realizing that I was now on the edge of coherence. An earthquake.

Another...

Sandy...

Sandy!

Another?

Another Propeller?

Given what we had done in our ill-conceived project, that we had produced a monster, Jacob seemed completely unconcerned. But when I looked around, the trees were no longer waving insanely. And somebody had cleared up the trail of bones across Jacob's grass…

"Another Propeller, Sandy?" Jacob asked. "Then I think we'll go into Lunenburg for a nice spot of lunch."

I nodded dumbly.

"But you shouldn't doze here in the sun any longer. Not good for you. Not even in a Nova Scotia summer."

Visiting Jason

It was dark. I kept stumbling on the uneven ground, but I carried on. It had to look as though I was on my way to see Jason, but was just confused, disoriented.

There was a whole string of ideas to contemplate. For example, I focused on my primary objective over the next little while, that I was off to see my old friend Jason, and from a number of practical points of view, that meant an early start. Hence the fact that it was dark. But there had to be some felt sense of uncertainty, a sense that things were unsettled, not quite what I expected. This had all been planned in detail yesterday, but now I was having trouble remembering the specifics of that plan. This wasn't intended to be upsetting in any way, but just irregular, as though everything had somehow become opaque, leaden, enclosed in some sort of spongelike indeterminacy.

My thoughts centred on a particular view of the world, and particularly of the previous day. I knew I had just dressed and collected the small bag that had been packed for me, but which I knew contained nothing useful. Given the length of my specified stay, the bag clearly was undersized. I just shrugged, knowing that all this would be attributed, as was the expectation, to a night of not very good sleep, a night which had been interrupted by a major, if short-lived, crisis.

It had taken a while to get where I was. That journey wasn't something I needed to recall; there were other things to keep in mind. Although everything around me was in darkness, and I had no trouble finding my way, I did stumble and grope somewhat. But I was aware, in a manner of assessing the atmosphere of the place, that there appeared to be no lights in any buildings. Everything was shrouded in a dim haze. The buildings were just shapes, and I was not concerned by the fact that I didn't recognize any of them.

He called my name. In his right hand was a lantern, whose glow must have been scarcely five watts. It didn't cast any light, and was really just a guide post, indicating something to aim at. I nodded, irrationally, since it seemed to me that there was no way he could have made out my features or even seen any movement. Indeed, I wondered whether the intent behind all this had been adequate, had been understood. It wasn't my concern. I climbed in and made myself comfortable.

"You're going to see Jason, are you?"

"Yes", I replied. "Do you know him?"

"Yes, I do."

I played my part, waited for him to say more, but nothing was forthcoming.

"I know everyone", he said, after a very long delay, long enough to cause doubt as to whether we were still in the same clip of conversation or if he was beginning something new. It hardly seemed important, even though any logic or sense of continuity was scarcely evident.

We were moving very slowly. It was peaceful, not in that comforting, reassuring sense that usually accompanies a peaceful mood, but in the sense that time or objectives didn't really matter, that destinations were somehow irrelevant. I wasn't too worried about any of it. I was just looking forward to seeing Jason again. The picture I had of him was hazy. That didn't matter. It was clear that we could reconnect and fill in any blanks, although I wasn't at all certain what that meant. Indeed, I was having trouble remembering many things, but somehow that seemed normal in a way that I didn't try to pinpoint. My expression would have reflected all this, in some way.

The water lapped. The air was damp and misty. The only other sound was an occasional squeaking or grinding. We continued moving slowly. I could sense my thoughts fading in and out as a feeling of disconnection came over me. It was not an unpleasant feeling. In fact, it was not a feeling that could be described in any terms that referred to any sort of emotion. A bit of stress in the background, as is always the case, but mainly a sense of generalized relaxation, not focused on anything.

Jason.

How long since I had seen him last?

I remembered that we had gone on a trip. When was it? About a year ago? It was difficult, for some strange reason, to reckon the lapse of time. It was quite a while ago, anyway. We would have things to talk about, later. But even as that thought came to me, I wondered just what we would talk about. I could feel my own facial expressions changing, showing now fond recollection, now perplexity, as these thoughts came and went.

I looked at the faint lamp, and could just make out the figure behind it.

"We're almost there", he said, without any preamble, and I knew I had to get ready.

A short time later, we stopped.

"We're here", he said, in his resigned and toneless way.

I picked up my bag, which now seemed much smaller, and rose.

"Aren't you forgetting something?" he asked.

My head was now almost completely empty of thought, but after a few seconds it was clear that the time had come to do what I was intended to do at that point.

I handed him the coin, and stepped out of the boat onto the dark shore. I walked up the slope, away from the Styx, as I was intended to do, then I turned and looked back toward the boat.

"Cut! And print!"

It took me a few moments to remove the dark contact lenses, something that made me stumble more credibly. The boatman was standing on the shore, smoking a cigar.

Bright lights now flooded the scene. I walked back to join the Charon character.

"Do you think they saw this coming?" I asked.

He grinned.

"I doubt it."

Along the Bay of Noto

There was a bit of fuss picking up the rental car at Catania, and we passed the time gazing through the arrival hall's huge window at Etna, half hoping for the excitement of an eruption. Eventually, being seated in the car, our bags stowed, we thought we had the problem licked. But our welcome to Sicily had just begun.

It was rather a long trek from the airport to our villa, a trek that included a good hour of hopeful turns into winding lanes, always leading to some place other than our destination. It was during that hour when the potential for murder arose, the likely victim being the voice that kept handing down hopeless GPS navigation instructions.

But then, finally, and having generated no corpses, we were in the villa, into the showers, and out onto the large terrace. It was some welcome.

In front of us, the land fell away over twenty metres or so to the Mediterranean, which stretched over the horizon toward North Africa. That view was framed close-up by several palm trees, a banana tree about five metres away, and an assortment of cactus types. A more distant frame was provided by the shoreline as it curved to our right around the Bay of Noto, shading first into mixed browns and greens, then softening to hazy blues and purples as the line of sight stretched away to twenty, thirty, and forty kilometres. Not only had we traversed the Atlantic, we had left a continental climate and descended seven degrees of latitude, fetching up near the southeastern corner of Sicily, a dozen kilometres or so south of Siracusa. Now, all four of us settled into a gorgeous sunny afternoon.

The banana tree caught my eye right away.

"Where are the bananas?" Teresa asked, her eyes and smile shimmering in expectations of tropical paradise.

"I expect that people keep picking them. Despite the risk."

A cold front passed over the group.

"Risk? What risk?" Teresa said, her tropical paradise just having been obliterated by an unforeseen typhoon.

"The spiders, of course."

"Spiders?"

Teresa shivered and checked for crawling armoured insects near her feet. Andy looked around, as though expecting large unpleasant black things to be dropping from the skies. Yvon just smiled inscrutably. They were all expecting me to say something more. So I did. All the human flesh on the terrace, except mine, was suddenly visited by a shiver of fear.

"Associated with the tarantella", I said, still examining the banana tree.

"Isn't that a Spanish dance?" Yvon suggested.

"Could be. But one sees it performed most competently in southern Italy."

Yvon rose, entered the kitchen, and returned bearing two bottles of rosato and four glasses. Somehow, the wine managed to disperse the clouds of trepidation.

We poured and raised our glasses to each other, and to Poseidon, whose contented underarm scratching was probably the reason for the mild swell coming ashore. I smiled and gazed at my wine through reflecting sunglasses, hoping to look like the subject of a Colville painting. I regarded the others. Yvon now smiled knowingly at me. The first sips of wine had transported Teresa fully to a safe and secure Sicily. Andy didn't really care. The sun was on his skin and there was a glass of wine in his hand, so he was equal to anything the world could throw at him.

After another long sip, I set down my glass and drifted over to take a closer look at the banana tree.

There was a short delay before Teresa posed another question, evidently concerned about a return of conceptual black clouds.

"What are you looking at?"

"Things that live in banana trees."

"What kind of things?"

"Tarantulas."

"Will you please stop talking about tarantulas?"

"Well. That's where they live. In banana trees."

"You don't even know there's one there. Have you seen him?"

"It's probably a her."

"Have you seen her?"

"But then it might be a him."

"Okay. Have you seen it?"

"No."

Our villa was built on land that sloped down from the public street to the sea. Access to the property was open only to the privileged, by means of gates separating the street from the property and its upper level parking area. Along this slope from gates to sea were patches of garden, surrounded by low walls to retain the soil, each of these patches being home to a profusion of sub-tropical plants. The villa itself rested on a plateau about halfway down to the sea. On the seaward side of the villa was the large terrace, flagged in terracotta tiles and also including a three-foot-high wall to prevent people doing a wine stumble into the cactus garden immediately below. Going down the steps from the terrace, one came to a large flat area where there were small drinks tables surrounded by chairs and loungers. From this area, we had an unobstructed view over the sea, and a good sightline past the deck that belonged to the adjacent property, and from there along the coast. Having this clear view of the neighbour's deck turned out to be important.

Among us, we had enough Italian to get by, but a discussion of anything detailed or subtle, such as tomorrow's weather, was beyond us. We found the locals to be unfailingly friendly and helpful. They were also trustworthy. It was our own primitive understanding of how things are done in Sicily, of the basic house rules in the villa, and why things were as they were, that produced the puzzlement and the hilarity we experienced all during the time we were there. I guess that's why we travel: to learn.

Siracusa was just a short drive from our villa, and although after only a few days we became old hands at finding our way there and back, almost every trip had some element of adventure. But it was worth every misstep and misunderstanding. Siracusa itself, Archimedes' city, and especially the old part called Ortigia, was utterly fascinating. I think we probably walked every street.

Our first foray into Siracusa included a few white knuckle moments. If you drive in Sicily, it helps to know that the message transmitted by any traffic sign is aspirational only. Drivers need to have a reasonable amount of actual driving skill, combined with the willingness and ability to engage in Sicilian four-wheeled poker, and a certain amount of pride. The pride comes in on those occasions when a momentary dip in judgment leaves its mark: a bent quarter panel on your car. But these dents, scrapes, and wrinkles are nothing to be ashamed of. They are badges of honour. They are also reminders never to make eye contact with another driver, and never to leave too much space ('too much' generally being more than about three centimetres) between your car and the next car. Most of all, they are reminders to expect that another lane of traffic might appear without warning, no matter how many cars there are abreast already. It's a serious mistake to assume that there's no room for another lane of traffic. The fact that there are already four cars abreast, plus one parked on each side, in a street that is six metres wide, is not relevant. In Sicily, there's always room for another lane.

Having arrived in Siracusa that first day, bathed in nervous sweat but grateful that we were all still alive and that our car was unmarked, we headed for a car park whose sign informed us that there were twenty-three spaces free. Already seasoned hands, we thought, after a mere forty minutes! Suddenly, a wiry gentleman loomed before us, making winding motions with his right hand. I assumed this meant he wanted me to roll down my window, and not the alternative hypothesis that he was miming the reload of a semi-automatic weapon.

"You can't park here", he stated in reasonable English. "This is a car park."

I'd like to say that I grasped his meaning immediately. In fact, it took a good hour to come up with even a plausible interpretation, which was 'You can't park here because this is a special car park'. He made hand motions that said clearly we should move away from the entrance to this car park that wasn't a car park. Fine by me. I wasn't eager to give him a reason to pull out the semi-automatic.

He said something about a tree. We had had our first lesson that not everything in Sicily is what it seems. We came to a tree, but that wasn't it. We came to another tree, and then just followed the car ahead of us when it darted down a street to the right. This street turned out to be okay, but it was a clogged artery, the plaque on the artery walls being double- and triple-parked cars. Weaving our way down this street, we eventually found a large car park whose sign said "Libero". By this time, we had enough savvy not to interpret "Libero" as meaning "At No Cost".

Once on foot in Ortigia, the threats to blood pressure and pulse rate basically vanished. We drifted through Piazza di Archimede, Piazza del Duomo, Piazza di Minerva, visited the Temple of Apollo ruins, shopped on Via Roma, peered into the Fountain of Arethusa, and scanned the harbour. We bought things. Lengths of lovely silk, covered in hand-painted Sicilian dialect script, meaning we knew not what. A blank papyrus scroll ready to receive our words of wisdom. A drawing by Archimedes (but the dealer didn't know what it was a drawing of). Nice things. Delightful things. Things that we would never use. We took hundreds of pictures, but looking at them later we agreed that they all fell short of the reality. I bought a book on Archimedes, one of my heroes from the ancient world. The book was in Italian. It took a good few hours for me to plough through it, but it was worth the effort. I half-hoped to see him galloping naked down one of Siracusa's streets shouting "Eureka!" ("I have found it!")

Somehow, perhaps through some linguistic fistula, this Archimedean image merged with the prissy phrasing that denotes leaving virginity behind, and that maybe this was what the old scholar had found.

"I've lost my virginity. I know I had it just a moment ago. Have you seen it?"

Or had Archimedes found something else?

"Where would he have found it?" one of the others asked.

"Well, probably under the bed", I replied, not knowing how prescient this speculation would turn out to be.

At one o'clock, hunger and the heat of the day said that we should press villa-wards. We did, but stopped along the way at a supermarket called Famila. There were hints that this was controlled by the Mob, but we didn't inquire too closely into that. We didn't want to be surprised, wheeling our cart along the wine aisles, to see someone point to us, and call out to 'Vito' in a gravelly voice, telling Vito to make sure he brought his 'piece'. Bottles of wine tumbled from the shelves into our cart. We marvelled at the massive jugs of wine on offer, which we felt should have been labelled 'Vino Blotto'.

We bought fruit. We found some nice biscotti. We purchased flour, walnuts, pistachios. We loaded vegetables into our cart, including beautiful clean leeks and assorted onions. We selected the wherewithal for a good risotto. At the cheese counter, I asked the severe looking woman for 'sei etti' of Maasdam. She lopped off a piece, and laid it on the weigh scale.

592 grams.

Her stern glare challenged me to argue about the missing eight grams. No risk there. Likely an error in the weigh scales anyhow, I rationalized. I apologized for my poor Italian, in Italian, and she broke into the most charming broad smile, and said something that might have been interpreted as 'Come to my place after work', but might have meant instead 'I understood you perfectly'. We paid, loaded our treasures into the car, honed our improving intimidation tactics in getting the car out of the supermarket car park, a surprisingly complex process, and then rollicked our way home.

Across roundabouts, where the last thing one does is look at any other driver.

Past the curiously named 'Albatros Hotel'.

Past the filling station, where we found that the slot for credit cards, which was the only way of paying, was covered by duct tape.

Past a dark and ominous rectangular hole in the hard limestone, which was probably home to a family of midget Cyclops.

Past the ruin that reminded me, irrationally, of 'The Three Little Wolves and the Big Bad Pig'.

Past the turning to Cassibile.

And then to the row of large plastic garbage bins, our signal to turn right.

Leaving the main road, which had room for at least twelve lanes of traffic, we entered Via degli Zaffiri, four metres wide and good for only a paltry eight lanes. To arrive at our destination, our villa, we had to skirt the 'sinkhole from hell', a compound set of massive potholes in the middle of the road, wade through 'Lago di Plemmirio', a giant body of rainwater that we feared was bottomless, and around a sharp corner where, it seemed, we always met someone trying for a new land speed record.

And then we were there.

We parked and unloaded. Cheese and wine were laid out. Excess clothing was removed. The most important part of the day began. Confirmation of this was offered by the two lizards, Castor and Pollux, who joined us on the terrace.

We had adventures. Some of them we encountered on our own. Some were laid on by Mother Nature. Some appeared to be just the result of 'the way things are done here'.

We visited Cassibile, home to what looked like a film set for wartime Italy. Home also to an amazing small supermarket run by Salvatore. Salvatore's arms pumped the air and he demanded to know where we were from, and then he began dealing with what he evidently considered our lifetime of culinary deprivation. Slices of sausage were cut and offered to us, although 'offered' isn't the right word, because refusal wasn't an option. We tasted wine from his mother's vineyard. He promised us figs from his cousin's garden. Olive oil came from another relative. Cheeses were a family specialty. We asked about fresh pasta. Salvatore was aghast. Sicilians didn't eat fresh pasta, he said. Only those barbarians to the north, the Italians, did that. He wrung his hands in apology at not having any *acetto balsamico*, but declared brightly that his brother had just made some and it would be here '*oggi*'. 'Oggi', we discovered, meant later today, after five o'clock, meaning that we had to return, meaning that the next phase of our education could take place, meaning that his irresistible sales pitch could be made once more.

We visited Salvatore several times, but then didn't go again. It's not that our education was complete. Salvatore's enthusiasm and persuasiveness at each visit meant that the drain on the exchequer was too severe. But he was a consummate salesman and an energetic human being.

The most important part of our education at Salvatore's place centred on wine. He made this very clear.

Holding up a bottle of white wine, he said "Vino bianco — cold!"

But then his expression clouded over. He held a bottle of red wine before us.

"Vino rosso — No cold! No cold!" Then something that sounded like 'Repeat after me!'

If we got this one wrong, it was clear that a large number of Hail Marys would be needed.

We couldn't leave until he was sure that we had absorbed this mantra.

Back at the villa, we slapped steaks on the barbecue and whipped up a makeshift ratatouille. Over dinner, we were heady from all the new knowledge being thrust at us. Images of Salvatore returned, and we challenged each other on whether the wine was sufficiently cold or no cold. For some reason, Peter Sellers joined us, and we began asking each other 'Does your dog bite?' and 'Is this a bomb?' Uncontrollable laughter led more than once to a coughing fit after food followed the wrong path.

It was on about the third or fourth day that we saw first-hand the ire of the gods. The wind rose. The seas became heavy, and then wild. Waves lashed the ragged limestone that formed the shore just down from our villa. The breakers roared. Spray rose into the air. It was a fantastic show.

We knew that Poseidon was on our side. We smiled, then laughed in genuine enjoyment at the show he was staging. His approval returned in the form of even greater tumult. But it soon became evident that someone's behaviour did not amuse Poseidon. That someone evidently was lodged at the resort immediately to the right of our villa. Specifically, his displeasure at their behaviour was aimed at the resort's wooden deck that sat on the rocks, about a metre above normal sea level.

Spray drenched the deck and slammed the chairs and loungers arrayed on it against the stucco wall of the resort itself.

We cheered at this display.

Poseidon smiled and renewed his efforts.

A large wave lifted one corner of the deck entirely.

We applauded and shouted 'Bravo!'

From then, it was just a matter of time. The deck heaved and buckled. Planks were torn loose from it and flew through the air. Then more than half the deck rose on a particularly powerful wave, came crashing back onto the rocks, and broke into pieces. In less than half an hour, the deck was no more.

This show brought out our thirst, more wine was opened, Dionysus approved, and that day we became the chosen few.

It was the next day when we recognized an imminent threat. We were running out of toilet paper. The cabinet in one of the bathrooms contained the last two rolls. We searched the villa, but found no other stashes. Before giving more business to the Mob, we called the owner of the villa. In short order, the man who did maintenance turned up. He was puzzled at our concern about toilet paper.

"There's lots of toilet paper!"

"Where?" we asked.

He indicated I should go with him. He led me to my bedroom.

"The toilet paper's there", he said.

"Where?" I asked, seeing nary a roll.

"There!" as though it was in plain sight.

I shook my head.

He moved to the foot of my bed, and lifted the frame to reveal all the toilet paper anyone could ever want, plus a large number of cardboard boxes, most of them empty. The immediate problem was overcome, but an enduring mystery was revealed. Did Archimedes have a bed just like this?

And so our two weeks passed.

We enjoyed the sun. We enjoyed the wine and the food. We enjoyed completely being in this part of Sicily. We laughed. But I think it was our own ignorance of how things are done there that led to our enjoyment.

Mostly we enjoyed the pleasant, helpful, and engaging Sicilians that we met everywhere.

Down That Road

These days, being an old bastard doesn't need to cramp your style. Not that I would give in easily to any perception of cramped style. But there can come a time when the enthusiasm of the mind, reaching out eagerly to grasp and overcome an appealing challenge, comes up against the wall of an old body's limitations.

At sixty-seven, I had encountered this unpleasant narcissistic shock. It was during a bicycle trip, along a stretch of the upper Danube. Gorgeous countryside. Fantastic eating and drinking. The thrill of knowing that I had not lost the ability to carry on fairly involved conversations in German. The satisfaction at hearing surprised pronouncements on the quality of my spoken German, even if, secretly, I acknowledged that people were just being nice. At least in part.

My German cycling friend Wolf and I had waved off the convenience of e-bikes, scoffing arrogantly at this gratuitous insult to our physical prowess.

Except that it hadn't been an insult, even though we didn't recognize this right away. Out on the trail, the flat kilometres sped past, our breathing settled down to something comfortably close to tidal air, the sun shone, and our confident spirits glowed. But it wasn't all a flat course. The first of the steepish grades came to meet us, but we soldiered on stoically, trying to hide from each other our indications of effort, which included a lot of ignominious puffing and rubber-legged performance. The fourth such incline, when we reached it, looked like the great eastern wall of the Jungfrau, and delivered its telling rebuke. We dismounted and pushed our bikes breathlessly up the last quarter of the grade, studiously ignoring the tanned youths who sped past us, and working even more assiduously at not seeing the two Germans, who were much older than us, overtake us at an easy pedal while offering a pleasant 'Guten Morgen!' and without having to halt for breath after the 'Guten'.

We didn't speak of it, but we knew that a judgment of sorts had been rendered.

The following year, there was no hesitation at reserving e-bikes. And that following year we tried something different. Starting at Münster, we had planned a route that incorporated pieces of five separate bicycle routes, taking us through places whose names resonated for me for reasons I couldn't pinpoint, but didn't examine closely at all.

We had checked into our hotel, found where we were to pick up the bicycles for the trip, then parked on the lovely patio for our first beer, the drink that initiated each of our trips. At trip's end, we would similarly have a valedictory half-litre. The weather was fine. The predictions for the coming week could hardly be better. I had been stunned by my initial view of Münster, and had already decided that the place invited a much closer examination. And Wolf had been in fine conversational form all the way from Frankfurt on the train, throwing contorted questions and expressions at me, intending to shock me out of the unenterprising dullness of English and into the full vigorous stream of German linguistic creativity.

"Not bad", I said, setting down my beer glass. Wolf just nodded, then shook his head in something that looked like wonderment.

"Not bad?" he barked. "Not bad? Was soll das heissen? Why is it that in English one says something like 'not bad' when one means 'absolutely bloody fantastic', and 'not so good' instead of 'absolutely bloody awful'?"

I knew enough not to be drawn into this little game. I sat, sipping my beer, perusing the city map, and occasionally looking up to examine our surroundings in a state of sunglassed cool. The route was marked clearly on our maps, a route we had decided months earlier at the end of a lot of transatlantic telephonic toing and froing over the many possible legs that could be included. But there would be no attempts at upfront analysis, no ecstatic fits of anticipation. Instead, we would take it as it came. These trips were things to be savoured a day at a time, as we sat pedalling and the scenes drifted past us.

"Noch ein?" Wolf asked, and I agreed readily to another half-litre. Our two fresh glasses of beer arrived by express courier, and we raised and clinked to ward off any demons.

"Immer wieder radeln!" I intoned, hoping to express something like 'Onward cyclists!', but not being entirely sure of my attempt at novelty, nor particularly caring.

The second half-litre joined its first half with alacrity.

"So", Wolf pronounced, smiling, the thud of his empty glass on the table sounding like a starter firing his pistol. "Etwas Stadtbummeln?"

I replied in three long sentences that said essentially yes, I would like to take a walk around town.

Wolf gave me the bent eye.

"German linguistic creativity doesn't mean an endless laryngeal flash flood."

A slightly puzzled smile, directed at Wolf, to indicate that he hadn't quite got the grammar or word use right, was just the antidote here, sowing doubt in his mind as to whether his English really was as good as he wanted everyone to believe. I flashed a second awkward smile at him, and noticed the shimmer of hesitation and uncertainty sweep across his face, reflecting a reinforced concern that he was not yet an accomplished linguistic mountain goat. It promised to be, once again, a good trip.

We walked around Münster, for about an hour and a half, and my initial impression was proven accurate. Münster really is a beautiful city. We found a good-looking eating spot not far from the hotel, enjoyed a superb meal, and were back at our hotel by nine thirty.

"Also. Morgen im Frühstucksraum. Um acht."

"I'll be there", Wolf agreed. "Breakfast at eight. Schlaf gut!"

And 'schlaf gut' is exactly what I did. It was the sleep of the just.

The following morning immediately after breakfast, we were off. As usual, there was good-natured ribbing as we advanced along the bike path. As usual, the German cyclists we met going in the opposite direction, and those we shared picnic tables with during water breaks and at lunch, were open and friendly. As usual, after just a few hours of fresh air, decent exercise, joking, the sun warming our bare arms and legs, and varied countryside drifting past, we had severed the links to the tyrannous quotidian schedule everyone wants to leave behind, and we became free agents in that great, privileged world of cycling timelessness.

Against a repeated background of fine weather and good company, each day was a unique canvas of countryside, architecture, food, and casual discussion with other cyclists. The towns and villages came and went, many of them calling out for us to take a closer look. And since it wasn't a race, we did take closer looks. Many closer looks. The larger centres also didn't disappoint: Senden, Hamm, Bergkamen, Dortmund, Bochum, Gelsenkirchen, Essen. And at length we were in Duisburg, the end of our formal trip. But we had decided to keep the bicycles for three further days to do some local exploring, and with that in mind, on the first of those three days, we set off along the bike path, heading downstream beside the Rhine.

Mid-afternoon. Something had changed, suddenly, and it wasn't a change I expected, given the scenery, my generally very relaxed mood, the food, the wine...

There was something in the air. The views over the Rhine, the delightful villages, the distant civilized rush of train sounds along both sides of the river, the beneficent sky smiling down on it all — that was all there, unchanged. But now there was also a dark and cold feeling that seemed to have swept up the valley. It was nothing less than a spiritual miasma, as if one of the more menacing characters from the Grimms had landed somewhere, folded its black featherless wings, and was now leering. Leering at me.

I brought my bike to a stop on the bike path.

"What is it?" Wolf asked.

For a moment I stood frozen and said nothing. The *something* now in the air had made a chill run through me, and the feeling of being afloat and without care had vanished, as if swept away by a rough north wind.

"I don't ... I don't know", I said.

But one recovers from these moments of stasis, and I realized that this one must have arrived because of a sign off to one side of the bicycle path, a traffic sign giving direction to cars on the road beside us.

Wesel.

And that word immediately summoned up another word.

Rees.

Both towns on the Rhine. Very significant towns.

All at once, I could see his face again, could see it clearly. It was a face lined and toughened by age and many experiences, by what must have added up to a hard life, although there had been better living during his last fifteen years.

My Uncle Graham.

He had told me all about it suddenly. Without, as I recall, any warning. One day. That day. A day in October, many years back, as we sat next to the woodpile, taking a break from sawing and splitting firewood. It was all there again for me on that bike path, and I was reliving it all. For a fourteen-year-old, innocently and happily cutting firewood with my favourite uncle, the change that had come over him so suddenly had been strange and dark and scary. And it came back to me now, here, standing next to the Rhine, came back with a force that was overwhelming. The things that filled my senses then were back with me now. That residual smell when summer has left. The cold touch but moody warmth of air flooded by golden sunshine, a slanting liquid light that guides leaves from their long home in the trees down to earth. The smell of fresh sawdust. The feel of twigs and bark snapping underfoot. The hollow clanking sound of chunks of seasoned wood as they are stacked in the shed. The call of those birds that have returned for the winter, chickadee and crow and jay.

And Uncle Graham.

The story he told had come out unbidden. His chiselled face gazing at me from what seemed a long way off. A face that was full of old pain.

I had no idea what had brought it out. Maybe it was just some feeling he had of a penultimate season. Maybe it harked back to an earlier time, when he did this same work, cutting and chopping, with his brother, my father, when they were both young. His brother. Who had been dead for several years on that day my uncle and I sawed and split, but was somehow back again. Maybe it was just an uncle–nephew moment. Had Uncle Graham been rooting through old photos? Had something reminded him of old comrades? Had one of those chilly waves from the past swept over him without warning, given him goose bumps, made his eyes sting? I don't remember that I had been prodding or questioning him. It seemed that it all just came out.

He had been here.

At Rees and Wesel.

As a very young man in 1945.

He had told me things, that day cutting wood, things that someone my age shouldn't have learned, about infantry friends, right beside him, suddenly falling dead, or having limbs blown off, and him not being able to stop, or say anything, or do anything. It was something I didn't understand, and I recalled clearly the feeling I had back then of being drawn nearer to him as a sympathetic close relation, an uncle now defenceless and in pain, but also seeing him for the first time as a total stranger.

"Jim?" Wolf said, touching my shoulder. "What is it?"

I shook my head, as though hoping that the moment could be dislodged, as one brushes a covering of newly fallen snow from one's cap.

"One of my uncles was here. At Wesel."

There was a silence. I shook myself again.

"What am I doing?" I said, sounding irritated, impatient. "This was all more than seventy years ago!"

Wolf stood looking at his bicycle, appearing deliberately disconnected.

I looked around quickly. There was a gasthaus about eighty metres ahead.

"I need a drink", I said, and I climbed onto my bike, and headed down the path.

It was still a gorgeous day. We took seats at a table surrounded by flowers, looking out onto the bike path, squinting into the sun shining from a glorious sky, and I ordered two glasses of beer.

"I'm sorry Wolf", I began, and then I explained the whole thing to him, about my uncle, about that day when he had told me things, about his experience of the Rhine crossing, about how he never returned to Germany once he had shipped back to Canada. Not even to visit the graves of his old comrades.

We sipped our way into a period of silence.

"I guess you had uncles as well, who…"

"Yes. I had three. None of them made it."

"Shit! I'm sorry Wolf."

"So am I. But let me tell you something."

And then Wolf went through his experience of Germany and a postwar young German coming to terms with the war. He was matter-of-fact. His description was spare, even, almost uninflected.

"You've seen the Stölpersteine", he said, turning to look at me.

I nodded. The so-called 'stumbling stones', marking places where one should stumble, stop, look around, think about what they meant and what had happened. I had known them from many past trips, and I had seen them everywhere during this trip. Little brass plaques, set in streets among the cobbles or the paving stones, recognising the fact that someone had been dragged from a house near the location of the plaque, and sent off to one of the death camps. They were tangible evidence of something horrific done on a huge scale, and evidence that that something had then been acknowledged, as a nationwide effort. Without any attempt at a whitewash. I had seen them in the streets during this trip, in Münster, in Bochum, in Essen. I had read the names, and the fates that overtook the people who had owned the names.

Deportiert Theresienstadt. Ermordet
Deportiert Auschwitz. Ermordet
Deportiert Majdanek. Ermordet

I then spoke to Wolf, wondering at what my uncle had told me that day, wondering why I remembered it all now. And I told Wolf about my uncle's face, a face set hard that day, and about his voice, reflecting pain but full of concern and affection.

"I don't know why he told me then, that day", I said to Wolf. "But for some reason, seeing just now the names Wesel and Rees brought it all back full force." I lapsed into silence and sat there wondering. Wondering about a lot of things, but mostly wondering about Uncle Graham.

And wondering why in hell I hadn't gently walked through the whole thing with Uncle Graham later, years later. There would have been time. Several years before he died. Time to get to know that part of him, that part of the world that had laid a black hand on his shoulder. That was also a world my own father had passed through, so it could have been a time to get to know my own father a little better ... an opportunity missed.

We talked more, Wolf and I, ordered another beer, considered how many kilometres we would have to go to find a hotel, said 'fuck the hotel', talked a bit more, and then just looked at one another.

At four that afternoon, we climbed back on our bikes and cycled hell for leather over the last fifteen kilometres, found a hotel, stuck the bikes in the hotel garage, had our showers, donned street clothes, and went off into the evening in search of dinner.

We had a superb meal that night, and although no decision led to it, we both got completely plastered. We laughed at stupid jokes, took aim at images of flies painted on the sides of the urinals, and reflected on the unreality of it all, on that enormous conflict, on the very different world Wolf and I knew today. How great a change just three-quarters of a century had made! But recognizing that the physical background of 'Germany', the place, what today was all around us, was very similar to what it had been back then, and its presence today, demanded that I not forget.

But before we descended willingly that evening into our slurred, tipsy, Bacchanal fugue, I remember thinking that I wasn't going to let something like that slip past me again. There was my friend Wolf, my close friend. We were linked not only by the unbelievably generous and forgiving face of the world we inhabit today, but also by that much sparser and darker earlier time. But now it seemed that something was incomplete. I became aware of a deeper personal reality. To know Wolf, really know him, I had to get a feeling for that time, in the same way he knew it. It was not until then that I would be able to feel the threatened curse, those remnants of brutality, bottomless hate, and inhumanity from that earlier period slipping away. Confirmation, of sorts, that I had found a path to understanding? Perhaps finding the means for healing wounds that had been time's bequest to me, wounds I wasn't aware that I had? An awareness that the past of previous generations belongs to us, and that it will exact its price, however much denial and ignorance we choose to throw at it?

I dozed off that night thinking of Uncle Graham, of my friend Wolf, and of being ready for a tomorrow that might look quite different.

Coffee

My target was Balzac's, a coffee spot in the Distillery District, and I quickened my step. The regular ritual of sharing coffee with Gerry drew me on. The warm welcome of that particular Balzac's location was always a magnet. And then there was the cultural, historical, and Dionysian tingle of that particular place: The Distillery.

As usual, this brought out my smile. And the delightful walk along The Esplanade just reinforced it all.

The Esplanade's many well-foliated trees always cast a lovely pattern of scattered shadow. But they also allow numerous birds to find perches, from which to add their contributions to the general symphony. The sparrows are the piccolos, although they have a decided metallic quality. Robins are clarinets. The voices of many children make up that atonal tonality associated with first and second violins. The cars passing in the streets add a poor rendition of everything from French horns to tubas, and percussion is delivered by slamming doors, barking dogs, and the trains on the track just to the south. Most people I know consider this symphonic metaphor an unlikely reach, but they just haven't tried listening to the world closely with the symphony metaphor clearly in mind. The more you think about it, the more interesting it becomes.

At its eastern end, The Esplanade terminates at Hahn Place, after Immanuel Hahn, a gifted local sculptor whose name, sadly, has sunk into obscurity. There's then a short walking path, close to where old General Simcoe built his first parliament, a quick deke across Parliament Street, and we're there, among the stone and brick buildings of the Distillery District.

I love bricks. They stay where you put them. Their range of colours always invites, for me, comparison to varied, strong, warm baritones. And the patterns that past architects were able to produce using just a few of those colours! Let's just say that my visceral reactions to bricks are complicated. But I do draw the line at going around claiming to get a high from bricks. I'm odd enough as it is.

Hence one source of my attraction to the Distillery District: bricks everywhere. Not only in the buildings but also in the streets. And behind some of those brick walls, the talents of people and *Saccharomyces cerevisiae*, otherwise known as ordinary brewer's yeast, are combined to create, to magic forth, from barley and other grains, liquids of various colours, flavours, and aromas that, well, you get the picture, I'm sure...

Then there are the old friends. I came across them again during my walk along Gristmill Lane. Not one of them is a person.

The big blocks of limestone in the buildings. The old delivery truck, a rusted-out freeze-frame from last century. The barrels. The elevated "Gooderham and Worts" passageway across the lane. And then the large, psychedelic model still, squatting in Trinity Street ahead of me. A quick glance up and down Trinity Street, flanked by buildings that seemed ageless, was as reassuring as ever. Heading off to the right, I made my way to Balzac's, which was occupying its sturdy little pumphouse as though it had been there forever, as though old Gooderham himself had signed the lease and welcomed the tenant to an indefinite stay.

Gerry liked sitting inside, so that was a good reason for choosing a spot outdoors. Giving Gerry a mild irritation, placing that bit of sand within his shell, always got the conversation going at an impatient canter. This condition can result from any of those life situations to which we are all prone, situations which represent a deviation from the ideal. In other words, that metaphorical grain of sand. And the specific situation? Well, there are numerous potential sources. Perhaps Gerry's toast had burned that morning. Maybe he had discovered a hole in his favourite pair of socks. Or possibly the offence had its source closer to home, for example, underwear that knotted in a manner known as the 'genital bind'. Or maybe it was a sun umbrella that won't stay where you put it. Or, in this case, unexpectedly having to sit outside. Any of these situations can tip Gerry into a state of agitated creativity. The result is always conversational pearls.

It was a beautiful day, and the high cirrus, the brilliant blue sky, and the gentle puffs of warm air signalled no change from that. I found a spot sufficiently distant from the gangway leading to the entrance to Balzac's, having seats that were comfortable and a table free of detritus. From there I settled in to watch the world, and to anticipate whatever it was that we would discuss.

I didn't recognize Gerry immediately, something that should have put me on notice. He had advanced almost to my table before I was able to strip away, mentally, the sunglasses that he almost never wore, but sported today.

"Where's my coffee?"

"Well", I replied, after a delay almost too long, a bridge too far, an apple too ripe, "I suppose it's still inside waiting for you to choose and pay for it. And a good day to you, too."

He sat and removed his sunglasses.

"We have a lot to discuss." This was an unlikely start for Gerry, a bit like Boris Spassky choosing the Ware Opening.

"We always have a lot to discuss. Perhaps you haven't noticed."

Gerry looked around, unperturbed, checked his watch, shifted in his chair, smiled a bit inanely at the sky.

"Today's different", he said, redirecting his gaze at me. "And what's more, I believe it's your turn to get the coffee. I'll have a medium please." And having said that he turned to look up Trinity Street, as though all matters relating to coffee had been resolved.

Just an aside here. Our conversations, Gerry's and mine, are a celebration of how to dispute the details while being in firm and final agreement on the basics. One area, for example, that never enters our companionable disputations is the sizes of cups of coffee. Not for us these absurd names, like 'tall', 'venti', 'ampio', 'énorme', 'unglaublich', 'cosmic', 'prodigieux' — a silly profusion of terms whose variety is exceeded only by their meaninglessness. What's wrong with 'small', 'medium', and 'large'?

An air of pleasantly controlled chaos reigned inside the shop. Joyce, my favourite barista there, was her usual smiling self, doing the job that she evidently enjoys a good deal.

"The usual discussion mugs?" she asked.

"Yes. And two peanut butter cookies please, Joyce. How's business?"

"Fine now", she said while mechanically filling my coffee and cookie orders. "Insane later. Probably very busy tonight."

"Billy Bishop?" I asked.

"Yes. Soulpepper. I keep waiting for them to ask for a share of our take."

"But you have spies, I assume."

"Who, us? Naw. Straight arrows, we are."

"Hah!" I barked. "Don't pull the other one. It's wooden."

"Wouldn't think of it. It's the combination of wood and nickels that I'm on the lookout for."

A tray holding my order slid to me across the bar. I paid.

"Thanks Joyce."

Back outside, coffee and cookies were distributed, and their consumption began. The cookies had been met by Gerry's smile of approval. But I noticed that he was examining conspicuously a sheet of paper on the table in front of him.

"An agenda for today? Action items for the next meeting?"

"Not a bad idea", Gerry replied. "Would make it harder for you to slide away from conclusions you don't like but have to agree to."

Our discussions don't have what one would call rules, but I guess one could say that we have conventions. These are things like never rising to what might appear as bait; agreeing as often as possible to propositions that are patently ridiculous; never cracking a smile at anything genuinely funny; and always laughing at any statement that appears serious. These conventions work well for us. They provide generous amounts of petard, good for hoisting. They keep us free of those desperate clutches known as Serious Discussion. They allow us to spring free of blind canyons and defiles that are too narrow. And, perhaps most importantly, they provide a means for scoring points.

"Given your concerns over health matters", I began, waving at the remains of his cookie, "I'm surprised that you don't worry about aflatoxin."

Gerry's slightly blank expression meant that he wasn't entirely sure what I was referring to. But he recovered nicely.

"Who says that I don't worry about aflatoxin?"

"Well, we've never discussed it", I countered.

"So? We've never discussed anthrax either."

"Anthrax", I said, nodding sagely, and gazing at a point somewhere in space just above the psychedelic still. "Now, straighten me out on this. Isn't anthrax a type of coal?"

Gerry tisked a bit.

"It will take a good bit more than having anthrax explained to straighten you out. But you seem to get some inspiration from looking at the alembic."

"At the what?" I asked, hoping for just the right air of willful obtuseness.

Gerry ignored me. I smiled.

"A common misconception", I said, offering a correction from a greater intellectual height. "It's what comes out of the alembic that's inspiring, not to mention inspiriting. But, perhaps you didn't mean alembic, since that's not what I was looking at. Could you have meant aleiptic" (an archaic word I had just come across and was itching to throw out, like a conversational caltrop), "or maybe alembroth, since I know you've always been fascinated by the idea of an alkahest?" Once again, I thanked my luck in possessing the Complete Oxford Dictionary and an irritating penchant for obscure words.

"Many things to be fascinated by", Gerry said in an unusually reflective tone, "not least uncommon words, although I doubt you could define any of them."

"Well, yes, but most people aren't much interested in words now", I replied, ignoring his challenge, and we let the silence stretch out companionably.

"What's on your paper there?" I asked, waving a hand in the general direction of the single sheet of paper, folded once, and held down by the copy of Shakespeare's sonnets that Gerry always carries with him.

Gerry looked down at the paper, as though seeing it for the first time, and hesitated.

"I've noted down some of the things we've talked about over the past while."

I looked at him, and I could see that this was not one of his usual gambits. The sun had moved around to the point where it almost seemed to illuminate his curly, sandy-brown hair from within, making it look like spun gold. His long, rugged face was handsome in a way, despite the distinct asymmetry of his large chin and rather globular aquiline nose. I would never have told him this, but his face, especially his smile and his blue eyes, exuded sympathy. We had known each other for decades, and he seemed hardly to have changed at all.

"I don't know what I just said", Gerry began, "but it must have been profound to leave you this dumbstruck. Have some coffee. Try for a kick-start."

I did take a sip of coffee, then looked at Gerry.

"I don't know what to say", I began. "We've been meeting now for coffee for more than twenty-five years. We must have talked about hundreds of things. I don't remember you taking notes at any of those meetings. Why start writing down stuff now?"

"Hey, I don't need a reason, do I?"

"No. But there must be some reason. And I'm going to be disappointed if you won't share it with me."

"Well, it was back in that hot summer of '93, and you remember the week after 'ol Sam struck a match on his ratty overalls and set hisself afire — "

"Oh, come on, Gomer. You can do better than that."

"Yep, I reckon I can. Now one of these days I'm gonna climb that mountain, walk up there among them clouds, where —"

There was a delay here, a puzzled look on Gerry's face.

"Where are you going?" he asked, no doubt wanting to know why I had risen from my chair.

"To find you a triple shot of bar scotch. I think you're having a stroke."

"No, go on! Sit down, you old fool!" He fingered the piece of paper, looked at it, looked at me.

"I'm writing a short story."

"You're — Aha! No! Not possible!"

"What do you mean, not possible?"

"I mean it isn't possible for you to create anything that's short. You try to write a short story, it'll ramble on for eighty pages."

Gerry went silent.

"We talked about short stories at one point", I finally said, after the lull had become uncomfortable.

"We did", Gerry agreed. "Talked about them for weeks. There was 'Leiningen Versus the Ants', and 'Mr. Articularis', and 'Signs and Symbols', and 'The Bet', and 'The Lady and the Tiger', and 'The Gift of the Magi', and there was —"

"Hang on Gerry! Hold it! Where's all this going?"

There was a delay here.

"Look around", he said, and he followed his own advice, gazing at the stone buildings along Distillery Lane, the brick buildings along both sides of Trinity Street, and the delightful pumphouse that accommodates Balzac's. I followed Gerry's example. It really is magnificent, what had been one of the world's largest distillery operations, repurposed to a stunning twenty-first century social environment.

"I've done some searching lately. I can't find any short story that's set in this place."

My years in the consulting racket had given me reasonably sensitive antennae, and they were twitching now.

"Well, I have to agree with you that it does seem this place would be a good story setting." Gerry and I have a complex set of unwritten rules covering our dialogue. Statements made by one always need to be met by a response from the other. Except, of course, where a response isn't needed. Well, I said it's complex. But in this instance I was expecting a response, and the lack of one just made my antennae twitch all the more.

Gerry had worked as a design engineer, and one day, decades ago, when I had needed a designer and he had needed an analyst, we just came together in a pub by divine intervention. After that, I had always looked forward to projects we were to collaborate on. We did so each from within his own corporate shell, but every one of our joint projects was memorable. During those years, I had formed the view that Gerry was basically a nuts-and-bolts man, interested in facts of all sorts, to be sure, but wanting things to be more rather than less literal. Not much of a reader, had been one of my early conclusions, and there had been ample evidence to confirm that view. Take our discussions of short stories, for example. Gerry was almost always Mr. Literal. And yet his contributions to projects were, without exception, rich and deep. The result of many years of experience, no doubt. The engineering world kept in a separate compartment from everything else? That had always been my view.

As I looked across at him now, he had that soft face of a dreamer, the look of a child wondering about something.

"So, let's do it", I said, acting on a sudden intuition. "Let's write our own short story that includes this place."

His expression, and the delay in responding, indicated quite a bit of mental stumbling.

"I'd love to, but I'm not sure that I…"

"I remember you telling me, too many times to count, that you don't know what you might be able to do until you try."

Gerry nodded, apparently in agreement, but not really looking at me. As I scanned our setting once again, it was the metaphorical garb of the location, the buildings, that struck me suddenly. A statement frequently repeated by our high school English teacher, along the lines of 'Only connect', came back to me: 'Seeing but not knowing, knowing but not seeing'.

He nodded a couple of times, perhaps acknowledging some inner conversation. Then he looked up at me, his face once more the usual deadpan.

"So. Are you going to be the corpse and I the detective in this story?"

"Me? The corpse? Only if I can narrate things in a lot of flashbacks!"

"Flashbacks? Who ever heard of a corpse having flashbacks?"

"Well", I said, "it happened in 'I, Claudius' didn't it?"

At some point the carborundum grinding of our conversation led to an agreement of sorts. And it felt good. Very good.

Part of the reason why it felt good was the realization that there was a facet to someone I had known for almost three decades that I was only just discovering.

I pulled out a pen, drew Gerry's single sheet of paper toward me, and wrote for a moment.

"We'll do a story in first-person singular but written by we two. How about this for an opener", and I slid the paper back to him. He scanned the sheet. A smile creased his features. He nodded agreement. As if orating, he held the paper up before him and read:

"My target was Balzac's, a coffee spot in the Distillery District, and I quickened my step."

Peaches

I'm afraid that I just looked at him rather dumbly.

But then I listened to what he had to say, thought about it, and the idea took hold in a way that I knew I couldn't shake, and didn't want to shake.

Working outside.

In a gorgeous setting.

Pay reasonable.

I could find nothing wrong with it.

On no previous occasions had I had any experience picking fruit.

"Not a problem", Ian said. "Sounds like you might be interested. All you need to do is say yes." His pen was poised above a notebook. He was serious.

I knew Ian from our class. We had studied the full course of engineering together. We spoke occasionally. Drank together occasionally with the usual crowd. But I knew virtually nothing about him. Certainly not that his family owned a fruit farm in Niagara. And here he was now offering me four months work, starting right after exams.

For some reason, I had the idea that summer work between years should be technical, somehow. But looking back on previous summer work terms, there seemed little basis for that thought. There was a summer spent as part of a survey crew, braving dogs, thunderstorms, hornets, and mosquitoes. I had spent several months servicing air sampling equipment in some very unlikely locations. Then there was the exhausting but lucrative summer when I worked in gardens during the afternoons, and then my nights from six to two in the morning were spent lugging garbage from a massive office building. Quite a stretch to link any of that to engineering. So, why not consider picking fruit? The real objective of working during the summer was to reduce the ultimate burden of student loan.

"Okay Ian. Put me down. How will I find out where to go, and when to turn up?"

"It's all in here", he said, handing me an envelope. There were three sheets of paper in it. Date, time, address, what to bring, what wasn't needed, it was all there.

"How many people do you hire for this in the summer?"

"Depends on how many regular farm workers we can get. But I look for people in the class who I think would work out."

I guess I must have looked puzzled.

"Recruiting people for this isn't as easy as you might think. Most kids want to stay in the city. Not many are ready for hard work. Many think of working at a fruit farm as either a joke or an insult."

"You're kidding!"

"Not a bit. You're one of just three guys in our class I think would work out. Looks like just you and one other are interested."

By then, I had had time to construct a rough list of pros and cons in my head. There were quite a few pros, and I had found no cons at all.

The more I thought about it, the more I liked the fact that Ian had approached me. First, I now had nailed down what I would be doing until September. Second, a quick calculation indicated that I would come away with a decent chunk of cash. Third, I liked the idea of being outside all day, almost every day. And fourth, next year would be graduate school, so this would be my last year for summer working for a while. Might as well take something where I had the choice instead of procrastinating until all that was left was a default option. Might as well choose something different and interesting.

That school year, my fourth year, had gone well. There was the usual month-long grind as we closed in on final exams, although sometimes it felt as though the exams were closing in on us. Then there was the succession of days that included little sleep as we sat those exams, sometimes two a day. At the end of it all there would be one late night of carousing and saying goodbye to many people I wouldn't see again, and then four days of almost continuous sleep, before vacating our various lodgings.

It was mid-morning on a Sunday afternoon in mid-May when I arrived in Beamsville and made my way to Valentino Fruit Farms. Ian was there to meet me, and he invited me immediately into the family home, where I met his father, was offered a beer, and very quickly realized that I had made a good choice.

Ian gave me a quick tour of the farm, which was quite extensive. There were the orchards, which seemed to go on forever, two equipment sheds, a partially protected area for storing containers of fruit from the fields, a large packing and shipping station, a staff bunkhouse, and a canteen for meals.

Returning to the bunkhouse, Ian said that the last of the summer hires would be coming in during the afternoon. All of us would attend a half-day orientation and training session tomorrow morning at eight, and then we would be split into small groups and be sent off to start the work we would be doing for the next couple of weeks.

"At eight tomorrow. Before breakfast?"

"No. After. We normally work from seven in the morning until six at night, but you're paid on what works out to an hourly basis, so there's no exploitation involved. But it is hard work."

"Are there people who don't make it?"

"You mean who just say 'to hell with it' and leave? Yes. Two or three. Every year. As I said, the work's not easy."

"So we work on a given task for just a couple of weeks?"

Ian nodded.

"The work comes in waves", he said. "Each wave lasts only a short time. So people shift from one job to the next regularly throughout the summer. We prepare for each task as it arrives. No point in trying to brief people on everything at once. You would just forget it anyway."

I climbed out of the Jeep.

"You probably should go and select your bunk now. You're one of the first ones here, so you'll get the best choice. I'll join everyone for dinner tonight. So, see you then."

And then Ian and the Jeep roared off.

The bunkhouse was functional and basic but clean, and the air was fresh. It looked larger from the outside, until I realized that it was divided into two sections, one for men and one for women. I picked a bunk near a window and fairly near the main door. There was a lock box at the foot of each bunk where we could store our things.

Pragmatic. Almost military. A little bewildering and disorienting, but that's true of any change. A step at a time. Dinner tonight. Breakfast and training tomorrow. Then the first day of work.

Returning outdoors again, I went to one of two picnic tables to the right of the door and took a seat in the sun. The air was laden by a blend of aromas, all of which I assumed came from the orchards. Birds were singing everywhere, probably with good reason — the fields would be bursting with ripe fruit in a few months, and the birds would likely be trying to get their fair share. My guess was that it would pretty much be all-out warfare between growers and birds.

From my seat, I looked out over gently rolling countryside, laid out in patchwork fields and neat rows. Peaceful. Inviting. And the locus of what I expected to be back-breaking work. My musing was interrupted on two occasions.

First, a tall, well-muscled blond youth walked up to the bunkhouse, introduced himself as Jeff, went inside, then came back and sat across from me. Before we could get into a conversation, a shortish young woman with medium-length brown hair came toward us.

"Hi. I'm Brenda. Just let me drop my things." And she went off to the entrance to the women's bunkhouse.

Jeff waggled his eyebrows at me. "Could be tasty", he said.

I nodded non-commitally.

Brenda returned a few minutes later and joined us.

"So, where are you guys from?" she asked.

"I'm at U of T, live in Toronto", I said.

"Queens", Jeff said. "I'm from Ottawa."

Brenda just nodded.

"And you?" I prompted.

"Oh! Yes! Guelph."

We talked a bit about how we came to be here and what we expected. Each of us had arrived via a different route. Jeff had something of a twinkle indicating that he might be a laugh in the pub. But even after just a few minutes in his company, he seemed to be radiating hints of something not so pleasant. The way he regarded things in what seemed an air of dismissal came at me in waves, despite my attempts to reserve judgment. And his comment on Brenda, someone neither of us knew in the least, was something I found unsettling. I'm well aware that first impressions can be misleading, but I found it hard to avoid the sense that Jeff didn't seem to be my kind of person.

We chatted until it was time to move on to what would eventually become known as the mess tent. There, I met three other students. There were a number of contract agricultural workers as well, but it was hard work striking up a conversation with them. Ian turned up and spent some time talking about how long the farm had been in business, how his family got involved, and what it all meant to him. It sounded as though he was the heir apparent, and that he looked forward to donning the mantle of owner and manager.

After dinner, five of us made our way back to the picnic tables in front of the bunkhouse, where we sat and chewed the fat for another ninety minutes. By then a little familiarity had caused people to open up more. Brenda was now talkative. But she was far from being just a chatterbox. Without having to make direct statements, her love of the outdoors became evident, as did her interest in people and what made them tick, and how she found her studies as a doorway into the world. I warmed to her almost immediately. Jeff had an endless store of one-liners and the dimple when he smiled now seemed more natural. It appeared that a communal interweaving of personalities had begun. At ten thirty, we all turned in.

6 am rolled around impossibly early, and it was some dazed faces that peered across the breakfast table. We ate silently, then trooped off to the vehicle maintenance shed where our first training session would take place. In terms of being focused and to the point,

it was one of the most economical sessions I had ever attended. Forty-five minutes later, we were dispersed across the farm to begin our day's work. They went fairly easy on us the first day, told us to knock off at about four thirty. By then, we were all struggling under the effects of a sudden surge of manual labour. But tomorrow would be the real thing, no mollycoddling. Despite the next morning's step into the unknown, dinner was a lively affair that night, and our expressions told us all of the communal surprise at how quickly bonds can form among people wrenched from a previous life's matrix and thrown together in a new setting.

It was cool the next morning, and I had stuck my nose outside to judge what sort of attire was needed. Light jeans and a fairly heavy short-sleeved shirt seemed just the ticket. The work wasn't heavy, in the sense of being strenuous, but it was repetitive and needed that odd combination of focus and disengagement. We moved through the orchard rows behind a small wagon, gathering up twigs and shoots that had been trimmed by another crew the day before. We collected fallen unripe fruit for disposal. There were weeds and clumps of grass to be cleared from around the trees, and bare patches in the mulching had to be covered. In a couple of spots, the elevation and the nature of the soil meant some selective watering was needed. I managed to find the sweet spot in these activities, and the day passed relatively quickly. Even so, by six o'clock, various muscles were complaining, and I knew that a fairly long and hot shower was needed to avoid a paralysing stiffness the next morning. We took our evening meal in silence, and I was in bed and asleep by eight thirty.

The days came and went mechanically. I got used to the rhythm, and soon realized that I really was enjoying being outdoors. The weather warmed, jeans became shorts, collared short-sleeved shirts became T-shirts that had even the stub arms ripped off, and we noticed that faces, arms, and legs quickly took on rich brown tints and that hair began looking bleached. We all learned to accommodate the work, and it was evident that sinews were tightening, hints of flab were melting away, and muscle definition was becoming more pronounced in all of us. Our evening meals became more animated. There was joking and laughter. Jeff and Michael, who was the straight man, had a knack for keeping everyone in stitches. Brenda, Carol, and Frances, the three female students among us, gradually took on a greater role in the group repartee as the last of the somewhat coarse male edge softened. But the work routine dominated our schedule, and the short stretches of off-hours activity had to fit in around that however they could.

A weekend routine developed as well. There was a strict rule about alcohol during the week, since each of us could be required to drive a small tractor at any time, so sleep and sobriety were requirements from Monday to Friday. We worked a half-day on Saturday and had Saturday afternoon and Sunday off. Most of us were far enough from home that staying on the farm the entire week was the only practical option. As a result, Saturday afternoons and evenings were a time for relaxing. Most of this 'relaxing' took place in Beamsville, and specifically at the Butcher and Banker. From the farm to the pub was a fifteen dollar taxi ride, and squeezing five people into a cab made this an entirely affordable option. The Butcher is a lively place, and Jeff soon became the soul of these Saturday evenings. But I noticed quickly enough that he was also on the make, perennially it seemed, and on more than one occasion I noticed Brenda or Frances having to brush him off fairly insistently. It didn't seem to bother Jeff at all; his after-hours world probably was a big sea containing plenty of fish.

Work shifted into a higher pitch as the summer advanced and picking of ripe fruit began. The yellow plums, apricots, pears, peaches, and cherries each came into season on their own schedule, and for each of these the window to do most of the picking was surprisingly short. There were also quite a few hectares of grape vines on the farm, but these were handled separately by people who really knew their stuff. It was during a weekend, as the picking operations got underway, that a musical car horn made its appearance late one Saturday afternoon. Jeff had set out that day immediately after work stopped, picked up his car, and brought it to the farm. He used it most weekends after that. But he seemed to use it for his own purposes, and it was never the means for ferrying any of us to and from The Butcher.

July drifted into August, and picking the peach crop was in full swing. It was hard work, but it helped that the heady scent of ripe peaches was everywhere. I found it exhilarating. During this time, our workload became quite heavy. The trees were weighed down by peaches, we had to select only the ripe ones, and this seemed to be a continuous operation. Getting the ripe peaches packed and shipped was a priority since they could spoil quickly, the pace of work was brisk as a result, and the days seemed to be very long. During this time, the end of each day saw a group of students who were pretty much bushed. A shower and change gave us a partial recharge, enough to have a companionable evening meal and an hour or so lounging and chatting afterwards. By then, snatches of repartee became relaxed and spontaneous.

"Are you going to go all summer without having your hair cut, Sam?" Brenda asked through an impish smile.

"Don't need to have it cut", I replied. "It just curls up out of the way."

"Lucky bastard", Jeff muttered, running a hand through his own straight hair.

"Long hair takes longer to dry after a shower", Frances commented without looking up.

"Who cares?" I said. "That's why evaporation was invented."

These occasions brought out the smiles of those temporary summer bonds, and I had been pleased to see that there were no truly unpleasant types among us. Evenings were marked by end-of-day languor. We talked about all and sundry, but I noticed that much of the discussion was on the future: what was happening next year at our various universities, vague ideas on what each of us wanted to do after graduating, hopes and concerns about a further future. We were all going through major changes, perhaps the first big rite of passage for each of us, without really having a good idea what that involved. More than once, I looked around at beaming, unlined faces radiating an inner glow of newfound idealism and unbounded expectation, but not yet tempered by the need to pick a definite course, to define boundaries, to aim at specific objectives, to know just when to apply full power, and how to pick battles. The child was gone but the adult was still forming.

I have thought of our discussions back then quite often. Some would characterize them as sophomoric. I always considered them important and essential, even if they never led directly to solid or immutable conclusions. Brenda often ranged back and forth across what seemed to be possible careers, lives she appeared to imagine herself occupying already, but without knowing how or why she had got there, and somehow still seeing it all from the sidelines. Frances loved reciting poetry, but the lines she chose indicated clearly enough the paths she saw beckoning her on. Jeff portrayed the clown, the joker, seeming to hide the fact that he was lacking a direction, or had chosen one but wasn't ready to discuss it. And me? I was in the thrall of science and mathematics, could imagine myself on the Nobel podium, and found it amusing to watch the eyes of the others roll. We were explorers.

That summer was long, hot, and mostly cloudless. And for our small group, disengaged from the world and occupying what really was a Garden, it was like a summer in childhood, something that wouldn't end. The rhythm of morning showers, work, dinner, and short but relaxed evenings were our staple of life. And it was perhaps for just this reason that a particular week in mid-August stood out. Spontaneous banter filled the orchards, accompanied by almost paralysing laughter. I can still see those bronzed, youthful faces, smiling, bent out of shape from mirth, eternally equal to anything the world could throw at them. As we set out for our half-day of work that Saturday, there was an unspoken conviction that the revelry that evening in The Butcher would be special. The half-day came and went. We hit the showers, changed into jeans and fresh tops, and headed into Beamsville.

Beamsville is no metropolis, but when a group of young people set out to make their own fun, the location hardly matters. At The Butcher, we had our dinner, joked over a first drink, and soon were all in stitches. Unfortunately, downtime seems to pass much faster that working hours, and soon it was ten o'clock and we were back outside.

It was a tranquil summer evening. Young cocks of the walk were revving the engines of their jalopies, displaying metaphorical plumage. Even though everything except bars and restaurants had closed, there was an assortment of people strolling along the sidewalks in the warm night, and we decided collectively to make a quick tour of the centre of Beamsville, before finding a couple of cabs to take us back to the farm.

There were eight of us that evening, and as we waited at a traffic light, another paroxysm of humour rippled through our number, set off by some clever remark, but then being propagated further just by its own existence. The light changed, but still in mid-laugh, we hesitated, not being in any rush. A cyclist turned the corner in front of us, but then there was a loud crash as he and his bicycle were struck by a car speeding through the intersection against a light that had already changed to red. The cyclist was lifted from his seat, bounced off a light standard, rolled a short distance along the sidewalk, and then lay still. For a moment, the car looked like it would stop, but then the engine roared and it powered off down the street and screeched around a corner.

Frances and Brenda screamed and began to cry. Michael and I ran toward the prone figure.

"Don't move him!" I barked. I placed a finger on his neck. There was a pulse. Dragging out my cellphone, I called 911, told the operator where we were and what had happened. As I shoved my phone back into my pocket, I began to shake almost uncontrollably. I still remember that pathetic form lying on the sidewalk. He couldn't have been more than sixteen. His bicycle was now a twisted wreck. Our shock at the whole thing was unbelievably disabling. One can hardly imagine the psychological impact of seeing a violent event like this up close. But the act of calling 911 seemed to have pulled me together somehow, and I knew that we would be asked to explain in detail what had happened. I began trying to recall everything that had happened. Brenda and Frances were now wide-eyed, clinging to each other, trying to deny a scene beyond their experience but that was right in front of them, real and insistent. Paul and Angus were trying to comfort them, but they were in no better shape themselves. Sirens sounded in the distance, rapidly approaching. A police car screeched to a halt not far from us, and an ambulance pulled up next to the fallen cyclist.

Beyond that, I don't remember many details, except that I seemed to be seeing one of our number, Michael, almost for the first time. Generally quiet, pleasant, and always having a slow smile, Michael suddenly had become pragmatic and decisive. We were all questioned, but the police, a man and a woman, seemed to spend more time with Michael and me, and although he was quite clearly shaken, Michael's responses indicated that he had taken in everything and was under control. At just before 1 am the police drove us all back to the farm. Brenda and Frances had gradually stopped sobbing, and looked stricken, but shook their heads when asked whether they wanted anybody to talk to. The policewoman looked less than convinced, and gave each of us a copy of her card and insisted on being phoned if anyone changed their minds.

Back at the bunkhouse, we sat at the picnic table for about half an hour, then muttered about going to bed. At about 3 am, my blanket was turned down. Brenda climbed into bed next to me, gripped me in a fierce hug, and quietly sobbed herself to sleep.

I didn't sleep. I couldn't. I knew something. And I had to decide what to do.

The next day, I went back into Beamsville, to the police station. It was there I learned that the young cyclist had not made it, that he had died on the way to the hospital.

Our remaining four weeks at the farm were solemn. A few people drifted away before the season finished, but four of us remained to the end. The work finally terminated, and those of us who had stayed to the final day exchanged long and emotional farewells. We all went off then to whatever came next for each of us. I was back in graduate school at U of T. I got a note from Brenda in late September bringing me up to date on what she was doing, and we agreed that I would travel to Guelph soon for a weekend. But something more draining awaited me.

I had never been involved in a court proceeding before, and I found the atmosphere suffocating. The step-by-step dissection of events was a brutal experience for me.

Then it was my turn.

"Do you swear to tell…?"

"I do", I said.

"Please state your name."

"Samuel Miller."

The case didn't last long. The police had testified, and there was a pro forma cross-examination. Then I testified.

I had avoided looking at him the whole time. Just couldn't. But I had to turn my attention to him when he blurted it out.

"Why are you doing this, Sam?"

I looked at him, but said nothing. Jeff just looked back at me.

"Order! Mr. Carter!"

Jeff ignored the judge.

"I thought you were my friend!" Jeff shouted. "You've wrecked my life!"

"Order! Order!"

And then I was outside in the harsh autumn light.

The whole business was very disturbing for me. But what was most disturbing was my own hesitation, the realization that I had come very close to just sidestepping the entire matter. It probably wouldn't have affected the outcome, because the police had a good case.

But I had seen the licence plate on that car.

I knew that it had been Jeff's car.

And I was stricken by the realization that I had seemed to be on the verge of keeping that information to myself.

In the end, I did see a psychologist. She walked me through it all. She was tremendously sympathetic and understanding. She told me there was nothing wrong with me, that I would get over the trauma. She gave me a few things to read, and said please to call her if I found myself in a state. And she was right. It all did subside. But it has never really left me.

Brenda and I got together regularly, became close friends, and for a short time we were loving friends. The trauma of that night has faded for both of us, but never did vanish completely.

That car, the boy lying inert on the sidewalk, the news that he hadn't made it, those things all meant something quite specific for me. I still think about it all sometimes, years later. What has struck me, looking back, is the contrast and the irony.

I spent six years in university, acquiring a body of knowledge slowly and at great effort. And yet, in contrast, that night in Beamsville and over just a few hours, I learned other things, fundamental things, wrenching truths, quickly and in a brutal way, in the teeth of tragedy and trauma. And this had been very deep learning.

Then there is the irony. There is peacefulness, a power and depth of understanding inherent in a peach orchard, something I was able to partake of without effort. Then right alongside that there was spiritual bleakness, the agonizing hours I spent trying to reconcile mixed feelings about Jeff, certain that in a split second that night a great wrong had occurred. I remember trying to convince myself that it had been the result of a moment of Jeff's youthful exuberance and inattention, but I couldn't deny that this had been followed by his decision of cowardice. I recall the searing feeling, being certain of what I ought to do without any need for reflection, but well aware of the fence I had straddled. I struggled in the face of a moral dichotomy that should not have existed.

In the end, I did the right thing, but the shame of realizing that I had to force myself to do it has never left me.

What the Frangipani Said

Paul wasn't sure whether he could carry on. The depth of pain was something he had never known before. He was numb, and for the first time in his life he felt incomplete.

There had been no funeral, just a memorial 'event'. Jerome didn't like the idea of a 'service'. And even that memorial had been small and private, just the way Jerome wanted it. But it had also been a celebration. There were accounts told about Jerome, things about him that were typical, unique, attractive, hilarious, engaging, bittersweet, loving. There were smiles. There was even some laughter. An ample supply of Tavel was available, a wine that Jerome had fallen in love with two decades earlier.

But then it was over. The last of their friends had said their goodbyes, and Paul knew that for some of them it would be a final goodbye, since they seemed not to know how to deal with Paul in the absence of Jerome. Paul himself wondered whether he would be able to deal with Paul in Jerome's absence.

Days passed. The first weeks dragged on.

Paul worked through the mechanics of dealing with someone departed. The will probate began, and it seemed straightforward, since Jerome's will was simplicity itself: he had left everything to Paul. No conditions. No codicils.

It took Paul the best part of a week to sort out Jerome's clothes and personal things. Most of the time Paul worked on autopilot, but even given that, he had to stop every few hours and do something less stressful. That effort did enforce upon Paul, however, a recognition and an acceptance of what had been and what was now.

Jerome had been his friend and intellectual soulmate. They had not been lovers, but they both recognized that many people would never be convinced of that. 'It's just how people are', Jerome had said, in his accepting, matter-of-fact way.

What was unexpected was the legal battle. Partly because it arose late, partly because it came out of the blue, and partly because it happened at all.

Jerome's family, who had showed zero interest in him while he lived, erupted after his death. They challenged the will. The challenge was before the courts for just a short time, but it was vicious and hateful. In the end, the judge ruled that the will would stand, that the family's behaviour left them no reasonable basis for a claim on Jerome's considerable savings, or his half of the house that he and Paul had shared.

Eight months after Jerome's death, the worst of the pain was gone, but Paul seemed to be simply adrift, becalmed on a vast sea of nothingness. He went to work without enthusiasm and worked mechanically at his job of insurance adjuster. He tried to keep busy. He met friends, he rejoined his book club after a long hiatus, and he went on Saturday morning cycling outings, something he had done regularly and loved. He read a good deal.

But the world was flat. The acrimony stirred up by Jerome's family left a horrible taste that wasn't going away. For the first time ever, his life offered no enchantment. He felt the unwelcome novelty of being lonely even in company or crowds.

Had Jerome's cancer been less aggressive, they would have taken a last holiday together. But before they could discuss where a last trip might take them, Jerome's strength had gone into an abrupt free fall. They were both aware, Paul felt certain, of a long list of 'might-have-beens'. Old haunts would have been possible destinations. But there were new places Jerome had always wanted to get to know. Paul knew what these places were, but it wasn't until early summer, nine months after Jerome's death, that Paul sat down one evening and began making a list. He wasn't sure just why he was doing it. Jerome was gone. What was the point? But looking back, he realized that that had been a decisive moment.

'Think a bit, then just do it.'

That had been one of Jerome's favourite statements, sometimes uttered as an encouragement, a few times as a warning, rarely as an admonition.

And before he knew it, Paul found that he had 'done it'. He would take a trip on his own, and he knew that Jerome would have cheered that decision. Even before he picked an exact destination, Paul knew roughly where he would go and about how long he would stay.

He obtained six months leave from his job, but even as he had read the boss's letter granting his request, Paul sensed the possibility, the portent, of something quite different. One of Paul's nephews was delighted to be offered the use of the house while Paul took his leave. And then it all just happened.

Everything went like clockwork. Calling ahead to make a final check on his accommodation and finding everything in order. The flight to Charles de Gaulle. Making his way to the Gare de Lyon. The train to Avignon. Seeing almost immediately in Avignon station the sign bearing his name, Paul Dixon, held up by the pleasant man he had booked to drive him to his destination. The car trip was short, it was prepaid, the driver was curious and friendly, and Paul put his French through its first real exercise in several weeks.

"First trip to France?" the driver asked in slow, clear French.

"No", Paul replied, and explained his history of travels and adventures in France over thirty years. In the mirror, he noticed a beam of approval on his driver's face.

"Vacation? Staying in France long?" the driver said, now in faster and more colloquial French.

"Six months", Paul said.

"Ah! You're an artist?"

"No", Paul said, smiling, and watching the driver as his glance flicked regularly toward Paul. "But I like wine, Arthur Rimbaud, and Victor Hugo. Perhaps that's why they let me off the plane at Paris."

The laugh coming from the front seat expressed approval for both Paul and a perspicacious French immigration official.

The driver made his way unerringly to rue de 8 mai, a small, delightful street in the south-central part of Saint-Rémy-de-Provence, and found the house at Number 18 without fuss. Its owner, a M. Chauvenet, opened the front door as Paul's things were being lifted out of the car. A glance at Paul's luggage telegraphed the query 'Just one bag? For six months?'. Paul's immediate clarification, in French, about always travelling light, seemed to clinch the matter. Inside, Paul accepted the offer of a drink, asking for a pastis on ice. They both sipped, and M. Chauvenet became more relaxed and expansive, as he realized that Paul was one of 'us' and not one of 'those'. He gave Paul a tour of the house, then handed over a set of keys and a card showing contact information in case of any question, problem, or emergency. He asked Paul if what he saw met his expectations, smiled at the positive reply, then offered his hand and departed.

Paul was tempted to go for a stroll around the neighbourhood, but it was now approaching four in the afternoon, and his next priorities were a shower and a nap. At seven he rose, pulled on shorts and a colourful T-shirt typical for Provence, opened one of the bottles of local rosé Chauvenet had laid out as a welcome, and then spent a half hour in the small but delightful garden at the rear of the house. There were pots of herbs, several clematis festooning a trellis, and a luxuriant but well-trained and trimmed bougainvillea that lolled across an overhead arbour in a bored 'Peel me a grape, slave!' pose. At eight thirty, Paul returned the now half-full bottle of wine and his glass to the kitchen, and set off on his first exploration of the central part of Saint-Rémy-de-Provence. Looking up at buildings and peering down side streets, he explored the area for twenty minutes until his attention was grabbed by the attractive lighting and inviting aromas emanating from a spot a short distance down a small street called rue Daudet. The spot turned out to be a bistro called La Cour des Frères. (No, Paul thought. Let's call it 'bistrot' to stick with French spelling.) Out of a combination of curiosity, spiking hunger, and an unexpected sense of anticipation, Paul pushed open the door. That really was when it started, the 'it' being something he had vaguely considered a break, a getaway, a release, but one that turned out to be more.

Paul settled into his rented house, and into life in Saint-Rémy, quite quickly. He had brought a selection of recipes with him, soon acquired more, and within a week he had added the very few items he wanted that were not already present in Chauvenet's well-stocked kitchen. Within just a few minutes during his first visit to La Cour des Frères, the atmosphere of the place, the welcome extended to him, and a bit later his first taste of the food had all convinced him that this should be his local 'establishment'. Within a few days, his entry into La Cour prompted a 'Bonsoir, Monsieur Dixon' welcome. The welcome became warmer as the days passed.

The experience one gains after arriving at a new location comes in stages. First is the period of raw novelty, when one is seeing everything for the first time. This can be very exciting, because the common and mundane sights, sounds, tastes, and smells of home have been supplanted by something completely new. Raw novelty wears off quickly, to be replaced by what novice travellers take to be veteran experience, but what is really just initial familiarity. Streetscapes become recognisable. A few new faces can be placed. Reliance on a city map drops away. After a couple of weeks, a novice traveller begins to feel encroaching boredom when all the initial novelty has disappeared. For the experienced traveller, these stages are raw novelty, initial familiarity, but then the beginning of what might be an indefinitely long period of growing intimacy and real discovery.

Paul had been in his new Saint-Rémy abode for a week. He had said hello to neighbours, several of whom complimented him on his accomplished French. By their smiles, it was evident that several shop owners now recognized him. And on his previous two visits to La Cour, he had struck up a brief conversation with the youngish man at the wine bar.

It was his second Thursday evening in Saint-Rémy. Paul headed off to La Cour for an evening meal and a few glasses of wine. As he made his way toward the bistrot, he noticed a spring in his step that he found both surprising and pleasant. As Paul entered La Cour, Marcel behind the bar waved to him. The place was quite busy, and he found one of the few remaining vacant tables. Behind the bar, Marcel raised an eyebrow and indicated the pastis bottle, and Paul nodded and mouthed 'Oui'. His glass of pastis appeared, along with a menu and a welcoming smile. The menu at La Cour changed incrementally, Paul had noticed, and he scanned it now to locate any new items.

"Pardon, Monsieur. Est-ce qu'il y a une place libre ici?"

Paul looked up to find a slim, almost sinewy, man a few years older than himself standing next to his table. The man had close-cropped dark hair, a pleasant face, and eyes that seemed to twinkle. His swarthy complexion could have been inherited Mediterranean, or just time spent in the sun.

"Yes, of course", Paul replied in French. "Please join me."

The look on the man's face changed from neutral to something else that was familiar to Paul but also something he considered complimentary, an expression that said "Ah! Definitely an accent not from here but one that I'm unable to place!"

"Canadien", Paul said to derail any incipient awkwardness.

Before the man took his seat, Paul rose slightly and offered his hand.

"Paul Dixon."

"Hervé Roux."

They both said 'Enchanté', smiled, and took their seats. Marcel came over with another menu, and Hervé indicated he would have a pastis as well.

They then exchanged stories. Hervé had been born in Marseille, had worked at various positions in the port, but had the opportunity to take a job in the commune of Saint-Rémy, and he stayed and had taken early retirement there.

"What do you do now?" Paul asked.

"I walk a lot, and I do what everyone else in Saint-Rémy seems to feel is *de rigueur*." Hervé allowed a pregnant pause to intervene here. "I paint."

The van Gogh effect, Paul thought, recalling that it was here the famous painter had spent some of his final years and created some of his best work.

"And you?" Hervé asked.

Paul explained as briefly as he could his recent loss and his decision to spend some time in Saint-Rémy. Hervé's face became solemn. Then he offered what appeared to be a statement of counterpart sympathy, saying that his life had been greatly simplified many years ago once he had left an unhappy marriage after eight years and made the subsequent decision, rightly or wrongly, that he was better off single.

"But that was all a long time ago. Old history", Hervé said, and a more positive appearance animated his face.

"And you?" Hervé asked. "We've had some famous people spend time in Saint-Rémy, but I tend to think that's all just something of a publicity stunt. Most of them don't stay long. So it's interesting to hear that you've decided to stop here for a decent length of time. Do you have connections here?"

"No", Paul said. "My friend and I had spoken a few times about visiting Saint-Rémy, but…".

Hervé shifted uncomfortably.

"But", Paul continued, now smiling, "I've always been interested in Saint-Rémy."

"Because of…?" Hervé prompted.

"Well, I know of the van Gogh connection, but I'm not that sort of culture vulture", he said, having to work to find a comprehensible expression for that term in French. "The place is attractive in its own right. It's close to Les Baux, to Arles, to Tarascon, to Avignon, to Orange. And I suspect that there are many more places nearby, less well-known but equally interesting. I want to get a real feeling for the area."

"How refreshing!" Hervé said, smiling broadly, and Paul wondered just how many times Hervé had had to grit his teeth while offering the most basic response in 'See Dick See Jane' French to someone who hadn't done even minimal background reading before coming here. "If you would like, I could show you around."

"That would be superb!" Paul said, beaming. "Thank you! I would love that!"

When Marcel came to take their orders, Paul selected the local version of risotto, while Hervé chose lamb.

"And wine?" Marcel asked.

Hervé looked at Paul, who indicated he should go ahead.

"Let's keep it simple, shall we?" Hervé said to nobody in particular. "A *pichet* of rosé."

Everyone smiled, and Marcel went off to fill their orders. The rosé and two glasses appeared within a minute.

"I've never been to Toronto", Hervé said, taking a different conversational tack. "Tell me something about it."

"Have you ever been to Canada?"

"Yes. Once. To Montreal. Many years ago. My wife wanted to go there, but almost as soon as we arrived she decided she hated it so much that we came home early." Hervé turned his wine glass on the table. "Let me be clear. Louise had some serious problems, but it's all in the past now."

"Well, let me give you a pocket account of Toronto", Paul said, wanting to move away from an area that was evidently sensitive even if long past. And he spent five minutes relating the history of a now large city which was nevertheless still in its infancy compared to almost anywhere in Europe.

"You make me want to visit", Hervé said.

Paul hesitated, and Hervé raised an eyebrow, sensing that some sort of qualification was about to emerge.

"Europeans generally do a better job preparing for a visit to North America than those travelling the opposite way. The non-aboriginal presence in North America is recent, not much more than four hundred years at the most. But it's the cultural veneer that catches many people off guard. It's thin. Going the other way, it's been my experience that many North Americans have no idea of the depth of tradition here, and how it pervades everything. To me, that is my bread and butter — the main reason I like coming here. But for many, it's invisible, so they go for the sound bite approach to history. Maybe they enjoy it. I don't know. But for me it would be much worse than a waste of time."

Paul stopped suddenly and blushed.

"I'm sorry, Hervé. I was ranting. My apologies."

Hervé laughed. "Not at all! I've never heard quite that explanation before. It's intriguing!"

Their meals arrived.

For the next hour, they ate, drank their litre of rosé, ordered another, and spoke about everyday things. At just after ten o'clock, they paid, rose, shook hands, and arranged to meet again for dinner two days hence. On the way back to his lodging, Paul wondered at how easy it had been to get into conversation with Hervé. In other circumstances, he might have been just a little suspicious that this sort of slide into familiarity would have been a way to gain his confidence, the other party pursuing an agenda that wasn't obvious. But in the case of Hervé, there was no hint of that.

The next morning, Paul awoke having in his head a perceived strong need for a project. But all in due course. A short walk brought him to the *boulanger*, where he picked up his baguette and had a pleasant exchange with the lady behind the counter. Back in 'his' kitchen, a café au lait, large chunks of fresh baguette, good lashings of butter, and a thick smear of apricot jam all told him that he was now really in France. After finishing breakfast and washing up, Paul went out to the back garden to do some watering and make a general inspection.

Another plant, he thought suddenly. Some statement of personal commitment. That would be a good project. A plant that I can look after. Something equivalent to marking the boundaries of my territory. Paul looked around the small garden. The bougainvillea and clematis were showy, but apart from the herbs they were really the only other plants in the garden. The clematis were located in a somewhat shady spot, where their roots would remain cool. But about two metres away, there was an area in bright sun, and enough space to put something fairly substantial. Back inside, a few moments of online searching gave Paul the names of three garden centres, *jardineries*, that were within a twenty-minute walk.

The first of the three was about eight minutes away on foot, and as it happened he didn't need to go any further. They had a good selection, the two people working there were helpful, and he walked around for about fifteen minutes. Off in one corner, there was a solitary plant, looking a little bedraggled, and without flowers, but Paul recognized the leaves.

"I'll take that one", he said to the lady at the cash desk, pointing to his choice in the corner. She looked doubtful.

"We'll have some better examples in stock in a few days", she said. "If you can wait."

"No. That one will be fine. I think it just needs a little care."

"Of course", she said, still looking and sounding uncertain. "I can give it to you for four euros." It seemed she might have been worried about post-purchase complaints, something that was unlikely for an outlay of just four euros.

Paul selected a small container of mild plant nutrient, paid for his two items, and carried them back home.

Home. Sounded odd. But at the same time not so odd.

In his back garden, Paul decided where his new plant would go, placed it on the ground in full sun but still in its nursery pot, watered it, and added a small amount of nutrient.

"All right", he said to the plant. "I assume you can understand English. I'll let you get used to your new spot for a while. Tomorrow I'll transplant you. Then we'll see what you can do."

He began walking back toward the house, but then turned and looked back at the plant.

"Let me know if you need anything."

That afternoon, Paul took a long stroll through Saint-Rémy, found a bookshop, bought a good book on the history of Saint-Rémy and another on the history of various towns and cities in Provence, took them home, and spent the afternoon sitting in the garden, alternately reading both books and dozing.

Having Hervé as guide meant that Paul visited every corner of Saint-Rémy, including places that weren't in his book. There were outings to nearby areas — Les Baux, Roussillon, Fontvieille, Vaucluse, Bonnieux, Avignon, and a half-dozen others. Hervé was very well informed, and Paul found that he had to do a good deal of reading to bring himself up to speed, historically and culturally, in order to make the most of the visits he and Hervé made. Each evening, Paul spent time in his back garden, which had by now become something of a welcome sanctuary, and after about a week, he noticed that his new plant was gaining strength, putting out new leaves.

More than three weeks had passed before Paul asked Hervé to drop by his place after one of their walking tours of Saint-Rémy. It was still mid-afternoon. Hervé acknowledged Paul's offer but was very reluctant. This came as no surprise to Paul, this sort of hesitancy being a continental trait. But Paul cajoled, spoke encouragingly in an informal way, offered a glass of wine, and eventually Hervé agreed.

As soon as they entered the house, Hervé was impressed.

"This way", Paul said. "To the back garden. I'll get the wine and a couple of glasses on the way past."

They were soon seated at the small table to one side of the garden. It was a quiet space. The stone flags under and around the table radiated back a soft light. A few birds could be heard, but not seen. The leaves of the bougainvillea and clematis fluttered gently in the occasional gust of breeze. Paul poured the wine.

"Santé!" he said, and they sipped.

"Did you plant the frangipani?" Hervé asked.

"Yes", Paul replied, a bit uncertainly.

Hervé rose and walked over to it.

"It seems not too healthy."

"It's much better now than it was just a week ago. I think it will do fine."

"Are you sure?" Hervé asked.

"Well, no. Frangipani won't grow in Toronto, so this is new to me."

"Sand", Hervé said conclusively.

"Sand?"

"Yes. You should put a lot of sand around the roots. They like sand."

They talked about this and Paul realized that Hervé had had some experience as a gardener.

"I'll bring you some sand tomorrow."

Hervé sipped the last of the wine from his glass and Paul refilled it. A period of companionable silence passed.

"How are you finding Saint-Rémy?" Hervé asked.

"I love it", Paul said without hesitation. "The history, the art, the people, I'm finding it all very much to my taste."

Paul noticed Hervé's odd expression.

"I've stayed well away from discussions of politics", Paul added.

Hervé sat looking non-commital for a moment, then to Paul's surprise Hervé embarked on a long and quite passionate dissection of modern French political outlooks.

Oh dear, Paul thought to himself, in a mixture of alarm and disappointment. *Hervé is really right-wing, and I've hit a nerve.* Paul was aware that parts of Provence are home to some extremist views, and he was now kicking himself for not being more aware of where people in Saint-Rémy stood. *Shit!* he thought. *Have I just blundered into a wall of hot buttons? How can I back up now?* He wondered where this might end, and thought of his still new connection to Hervé, someone he had come to regard as a friend, and the risk of all that just snapping like a dead twig. Paul fretted at a level of anxiety that he had trouble reconciling.

"...and it seems to be just a one-way course", Hervé said, shaking his head. "More than once I've thought of leaving."

"What?" Paul said, coming back to the present with a thud. "Leaving Saint-Rémy?"

"Well, not really. Saint-Rémy itself is something of an oasis of liberalism in a larger area that's extremist. It's this region that's the problem. All around us is Le Pen country. I find their ideas very hard to stomach."

"So you're not a Le Pen follower?"

"Good God, Paul! No! Of course not!"

Relief swept over Paul, and he smiled and poured the rest of the wine.

"Hungry?" he asked, as he raised his glass.

"Yes", Hervé said, appearing also to be eager to move away from a conversational black hole. That evening in La Cour, they had one of their more animated dinner discussions, and then parted on a very warm handshake, but not before Hervé made arrangements to deliver his sand the next day.

The following morning, Hervé knocked on Paul's door, and they both trooped out to the garden. In practised expertise, Hervé dug out around the roots of the frangipani and put the sand in place, explaining during this operation the need for great care to be taken to protect the frangipani's delicate roots. Some watering, the addition of a little more nutrient, and Hervé declared it all now to be in the hands of the gods.

The days flew by. Paul barely bothered to keep track of them. His knowledge of Saint-Rémy and some of the surrounding area was now becoming detailed, and he revelled in that. About a week after the sand transfusion, the frangipani had risen comfortably into Provençal vigour. Hervé visited the back garden regularly, smiled at the plant's progress, and he and Paul enjoyed what had become very companionable time spent talking about things in general.

The three-month mark passed. Apart from inquiring of Chauvenet about a possible extension to his stay, Paul deliberately chose to ignore this halfway point, even though he knew he was now on the slope that would lead back home.

'Home'.

Home indeed. 'Where is home?' he had begun asking himself.

It was the day they returned from a second visit to the spring at Vaucluse. Paul had read a good deal more about Petrarch, and had wanted to fix in his mind some of the connection between the spring and his now altered view of both the place and the famous poet.

He and Hervé were in Paul's back garden once again, and before heading off that evening for another meal together, Paul had produced a small cheese plate to go with the rosé. They sipped and nibbled.

"Maybe we could speak the English a little sometime", Hervé said hesitantly and in a heavy accent, after a long period of silence.

Paul looked up in utter astonishment, but then smiled encouragingly when he saw the mix of trepidation and earnestness on Hervé's face.

"By all means", Paul said slowly in English. "But why?"

From Hervé's expression, Paul recognized a fierce internal struggle to find the words.

"Why not? I need ... I want to be different. Political ... I'm already some... eu... much different... or... I mean... not like...."

Paul gave Hervé a beaming smile and refilled their wine glasses.

"Hervé, please feel free to speak or to ask me anything in English, whenever you wish."

Hervé smiled back. "I think that's enough for now", he said, relaxing into French and reaching for his wine glass in what appeared to be the eagerness of both confidence and relief.

They finished the cheese and their wine. It was not yet seven o'clock, and they agreed to meet at La Cour for dinner at eight thirty. Paul cleared away the glasses, empty bottle, plates, and napkins, then returned to sit in his garden and think.

His garden.

I've been here long enough now, Paul said to himself, for the initial bloom to have gone from the fruit.

He thought it all through carefully.

I need more time, he thought. Another six months.

There was a letter to write. An email message to send. A confirmation with Chauvenet. And a few telephone calls to make. But even as he thought about what he was on the verge of doing, Paul felt comfortable. It felt right.

He watered the frangipani once more, and looked closely at it. From a sad and struggling thing a few months ago, it was now strong, healthy, in full leaf, and had a dozen gorgeous blossoms.

"The flower of welcome."

Paul looked around to see who had spoken. He was alone in his garden.

"Just do it. Hervé is worth taking time over."

It was Jerome's voice. Gentle. Patient. Infinitely kind.

"I'll say goodbye now, Paul."

Lumley, Carl, and Me

As the hour to leave school approached, I always became anxious about hockey. We had to fit in hockey between piano practice and dinner, and that was one of my life's big challenges. Because it seemed there was never enough time.

"Hey Norm! Wait for me!"

Stan was the same age as me. Six. A happy kid, short, a bit overweight, but easy to talk to. He made everybody smile. I liked him, but he always wanted to talk to me at the wrong time, always when I was in a hurry.

I turned and waited for a moment. Stan was struggling through the snow, his features and signature gait recognizable anywhere. Head slightly to one side, big smile, always a runny nose, shoulders swinging as he walked, a long stride that made him bob up and down.

There had been only about four inches of new snow that day. In school, we watched it come down through the classroom window. It was this snow that Stan was working against. I don't know why, but he always seemed to like sliding one boot through the snow.

"Wait up!"

"Okay, I'm waiting Stan."

On my walk to and from school, something that took about half an hour, I went by Stan's family's house. He lived in a house made of concrete blocks. The house had been built originally by the quarry company. The quarry company blasted limestone, and then crushed some of it to gravel and made some into cement. Stan's father had bought the house during one of the quarry company's crises. My father said the quarry company went through a crisis every couple of years. I knew what a crisis was. It happened when the quarry company couldn't get enough dynamite and had to stop work for a while. I wasn't surprised at this. Dynamite is really hard to make. I tried making some one summer in our back yard. It didn't work. I think it was probably too warm that year.

While Stan was still some distance away, he was talking to me.

"Do you want to have a snowball fight, Norm?"

"No. The snow's not packy."

"We could use some warm water."

"No. Too much trouble. Besides, I need to do piano practice."

Stan caught up to me and we began walking together. But almost immediately I started pulling ahead of him.

"Not so fast, Norm. I can't keep up."

"That's because you slowed down."

"Did not."

I let Stan catch up to me, then we walked together, but once again I started pulling away.

"I can't wait for you Stan. I need to get home."

"Well ... Okay."

We were almost at Stan's house anyway. I waved to Stan and said I'd see him tomorrow.

"Bye Norm!" Stan waved wildly, as though I was on board the Queen Mary, away off in the distance.

"Bye Stan."

Then I really picked up the pace.

It wasn't dark. It was just that gloomy light coming in during the late afternoon, at the end of January, through a heavily overcast sky. We had already seen a lot of snow that winter. That was good for road hockey, to replace snow the plough removed and car tires made rough and irregular. But more snow was also not good, because it had to be shovelled from the path from the house to the garage, and from the drive leading from the garage out to the road. Where we lived, the road was straight and flat, so they never sprinkled sand or salt on it, except for that one time. I wanted to write to the village and complain, ask them to come and collect their sand and salt off the road, because it made the puck do weird things when we played road hockey. But my father wouldn't help write a letter. I asked my mother if he couldn't write very well, if that was the problem.

I always liked winter. Well, all except for one thing. My nose runs a lot, and it ran down onto my upper lip on account of me being told all the time not to sniff. So, I didn't sniff. I just licked my upper lip. But this made my lips wet, and raw, and red. It was something my mother called Chap's lips. I had no idea who Chap was, but he had a lot to answer for.

Usually, I got home from school at about four thirty. I needed to practise piano for at least half an hour. My mother sat with me for the first few minutes of practice, and occasionally she would tell me to slow down. I'm not sure how she worked out what I was doing. It's like this, see. In half an hour, I can strike a lot of notes. I don't really know how many, because I can't play and count at the same time. But it must be more than ten thousand notes. If I play faster, that means I can strike maybe twenty thousand notes in half an hour, so then I should be able to finish my practice after only about fifteen minutes. I was sure of this, because I'm good at arithmetic.

My mother thought there was something wrong with that argument, and I know why. She's not very good at arithmetic. But often she would let me stop after twenty-five minutes.

I had this worked out. The less time I spent at the piano, the more time I had for road hockey. We had to stop playing road hockey at six thirty, because that's when we ate. Every night, at the same time. So, if I hurried home from school, quickly took off my boots, mitts, and coat, and rushed through my piano practice, I could have as much as an hour and ten minutes for road hockey.

Out into the gloom I would go, my hockey stick over my shoulder, two pucks in my pocket. It was often snowing lightly. There was a single streetlight just up the road from our place, and most nights the snow on the road and among the trees along the road would wink and sparkle in the glow from that streetlight.

But the streetlight was perfectly placed. It was midway between our place and Carl's place. Carl and I would meet on the road, and our game would begin.

The snow formed a halo around the streetlight, a sign that somebody up there, somewhere above the clouds, enjoyed our games of road hockey. It was a bit like a rainbow, I guess, a sign that someone was watching our hockey games and smiling. The snowbanks on the sides of the road, never less than two or three feet high, were the boards to our rink. We had only one goal, and that was defined by two of Carl's father's old work boots.

Carl was nine years older than me, so he was a big kid. He worked at Archie Black's gas station where he was a very good mechanic, but he did everything else as well. He stopped being a mechanic when mechanics all had to be licensed and Carl couldn't pass the test. Archie said there was no way he would get rid of Carl. He worked hard and he understood any kind of machine. I think Carl did a lot of work on cars when nobody was looking.

His blue eyes were what most people talked about. I asked my mother one time why people had this thing about blue eyes. My eyes are pale blue, but Carl's are bright blue. My mother just mumbled something about people liking blue eyes, for some reason. My mother's eyes weren't blue, but I'm sure that wasn't important.

The thing I think everyone should have noticed about Carl was his hair. It was yellow, but the important thing was that it always looked messed up, even right after he had just combed it. Carl didn't care.

We always started our game the same way. I would begin in the net, and Carl would shoot the puck from about twenty yards out. I managed to stop most of his shots.

After about fifteen minutes of that, the real game would start. Carl was in the net, and I was all the other players. Carl was also the announcer, either Foster Hewitt or Danny Gallivan, two guys that Carl seemed to know but I had never met. As well as being the entire opposing team, I was also the referee.

I looked at Carl. He nodded and began his commentary.

'It's a capacity crowd here tonight in Maple Leaf Gardens. We expect a fast game. Lumley is in goal, banging his stick on the ice, eager to get going.'

The first time I heard Carl say the name Lumley I hadn't any idea what he was talking about. But there was no way I would admit that to him.

"Who's Lumley?" I asked my dad that same evening.

"Lumley? Where did you hear that?"

"From Carl."

"Ah!" my father said smiling. "That's Harry Lumley. Old Apple Cheeks. He was an NHL goalie. Long time ago. One of the best. Carl gets that from his father. Harry Lumley was his father's favourite hockey player."

It was time to start the game. I dropped the puck.

"And we're off", the announcer said. "The puck is grabbed right away by the Bruins' centre. He's into the Leafs' zone. Tries to move past the defence. Over the blue line. Turns. Moves back in front of the goal."

In fact, I was still stickhandling my way down the road. Carl was between the two old boots, crouching down, calling the play that he imagined was happening, hockey stick in front of his feet, his gloved left hand raised, ready to snatch the flying puck from the air in the unlikely event that I could lift it more than about a foot. I haven't made a shot yet. I'm dodging make-believe defencemen, twisting and weaving, closing in on the net.

"A quick pass to the Bruins' right wing. Ohh! The right wing just avoids a check. There's going to be a penalty here, but the referee waves the play to go on. Along the boards. The right wing goes into the corner. He stickhandles. He twists and turns."

Carl's commentary really had nothing to do with what was actually happening on the road, but I didn't care. This was road hockey!

"And now a pass along the boards. Behind the net. The Bruins' left wing takes the puck. He's wide open! He fans a shot! Here it is! A wrist shot! Oh, and Lumley makes the save! Harry Lumley. Hangs onto the puck. And the referee calls the play."

I had been the left wing Bruin in Carl's commentary, and now Carl smiles, passes the puck back to me, I move away down the road again, getting ready for the next play.

"We're ready to start again. The two teams take their places. To the left of Lumley. Behind the Leafs' blue line. Here's the faceoff. The Bruins' centre gets the puck right away. He races back and around. Misses a check. Now he's right in front of the Leafs' net! He shoots! And Lumley makes the save again."

This time it was me who made the shot, a real shot, and Carl made the save.

Every night, Carl did his running commentary. And every night, that commentary was a little different, except for one detail.

Lumley always made the save.

Even when I managed to get the puck between the boots and past Carl, Lumley still made the save.

This would go on for as long as I could stay out.

There was drama along the boards.

There were players fighting for the puck in a corner.

There were faceoffs.

And Lumley was always there pulling pucks from the air like flies.

If we were lucky, we could go almost an hour without having to move to one side to let a car past. All the neighbours knew we were out there, me and Carl, having our nightly game of road hockey.

When it was snowing heavily, the game became very interesting. The puck would go missing, and I'd have to sweep my stick across the road looking for it, concealed somewhere in a small hillock of snow. On rare occasions, we would need to move off the road completely, when the snow plough came along.

On wet days, playing road hockey was less fun because of the slush, but we were out there anyway. On really clear cold nights, we were there as well, the snow squeaking at a different pitch depending on how low the temperature got. But the best nights were the nights without wind, when it was neither wet nor too cold, and a light snow was filtering down. Snowflakes would collect on my eyelashes. Carl and I would both laugh. Snow falling past the streetlight would wink and sparkle. Carl's big smile filled the air, and even when it was dark, full night being upon us, we didn't care. We played on.

Occasionally, when I was tired of dodging Leafs defencemen and Lumley had made hundreds of incredible saves, we would stop for a moment, Carl and me, catch our breath, look at the snow falling out of what seemed an infinite black night. And I would look up and admire the way the pine trees held out their huge hands, palms up, and welcomed the falling snow. But then the referee would call for play to resume. I would station myself in the road about twenty feet from Carl. He would bang his stick on the ice. Lumley wanting to get back in the game.

At some point, every evening, when it was almost time for me to stop and come in for dinner, I knew my father would come and stand at the edge of our house and watch us play. I think he also liked Carl's running commentary, because every once in a while I would hear his soft chuckle as Carl uttered his loud, admiring, and victorious declaration that Lumley, our hero, the invisible third guy who was always present at our games, had made another impossible save.

Then it would be time for me to go in for dinner. Carl would collect the boots, our goal posts, wave at my father, and sing out his cheerful 'Bye' before heading home.

I'm standing out in the road again. But it's not the same now. Partly because it's the middle of summer. Partly because I'm now in my mid-forties, and I haven't played road hockey here with Carl for more than thirty years. Partly because my parents moved into town a few years ago to live closer to me, my wife Claire, and our three kids, now teenagers, soon to move out.

Carl doesn't live here anymore either. After his parents died, he moved to Lindsay and now operates his own taxi company. But the big pine trees are still there. There are more and better streetlights now, and one of them still beams down on the spot where we placed the old boots, where I took those shots on goal, where Carl broadcast his commentary, and where Lumley made all those saves.

I kept the two pucks we used to play with. They're nicked and battered now, but I still look at them occasionally.

I never met Harry Lumley. He stopped playing hockey before I was born. But I can still remember the cry that enlivened so many evenings for Carl and me:

"Oh! And Lumley makes the save!"

Lost Friends

I

It was raining the afternoon we moved the railway station.

That event was the culmination of a long and unexpected shift in my outlook. But significant though it was, the station move easily took second place, over the long term, to something else, a chance discovery that forged a link between my sleepy home village and a fiery hellhole in France.

In the course of pursuing where some of the furnishings in the old station had gone, before the building was jacked up and ready to be loaded onto the large flatbed, I had found a war medal, almost a hundred years old. And in retrospect it might have been better if that discovery had been made at a different time, or by someone other than me.

But it happened the way it happened. I had found it, and having done so I couldn't unfind it.

The old railway station in Coboconk turned out to be, unexpectedly, a memory catalyst for me. But it was a long path leading to the point where that catalyst would ignite a reaction. I had to be drawn back to Coboconk first.

As everyone does, I have flashbacks. Mine are short-lived, and can begin almost anywhere. There were lots of situations, events, scenes, from my childhood and boyhood that would come back to me.

For example, me and my bicycle.

In the days when steam trains still pulled into the village, I would ride as fast as I could on my bicycle to see the great pufferbelly before it did a one-eighty on the turntable and headed back down the tracks. I remember a whole constellation of images: the locomotive sitting there huffing impatiently, the sweetish, acrid smell of coal smoke, the heavy dampness of the steam it left in its wake. The loud toot from its whistle — a sound so deep and powerful that I could feel it in my chest — as the engine driver announced they were ready to depart. And then the first exciting chuff as it set off again, soon to pick up speed and vanish around the long curve about a half mile to the west.

I still have a snapshot memory, from somewhere in the mid-twentieth century, of a crowd in the station waiting room, dozens of people ready to catch the next train to Lindsay.

The biggest change to this picture, as far as I'm concerned, occurred when diesel locomotives replaced the great, black, fire-breathing beasts, machines which came to embody or reflect metaphorically so many other things.

And then, as quickly as they had appeared, these clusters of memories would vanish.

I left Coboconk in 1969, expecting never to return. My siblings were all about to fledge, my mother was about to sell the family home, such as it was, and by that time my father had been lying peacefully for six years in Pinegrove Cemetery near Norland. In 1969, Coboconk was for me a symbol of poverty, struggle, and in general something I wanted to leave behind in a hurry.

It's odd how things change. For me, a kid from the sticks, the big changes arrived in a lump over a period of about ten years: the excitement of entering and graduating from university, landing a series of good jobs, being married, beginning to travel quite a bit, becoming a seasoned consultant all too familiar with the insides of airplanes and chain hotels. And then returning from a business trip one day to find a Dear John letter telling me that my wife was now shacked up in Oregon. By then, I probably spared even less thought for Coboconk than at any time in the past, and that likely wouldn't have changed had it not been for one chance encounter.

It happened at the end of another long but successful out-of-town consulting trip. By the time I unlocked the door to my exquisite Market Street dwelling, it was dark, almost ten o'clock, and I was glad to be home. Walking through to the large bedroom, I gave a sigh of relief and welcome, and threw my suitcase and briefcase down next to the bed. It had been more than a full working day since a scratch lunch at eleven thirty, and I decided that a quick shower followed by a pub meal offered the fastest route back to civilization. Ten minutes later, showered and changed into my fatigues (jeans and old sweater), I walked into The Cocked Hat, a funky pub two minutes from my place that offers good beer, competently cellared, and a menu covering everything from pearly-gate culinary innocence and holiness to short-term heart failure.

The fate of my first pint was the stuff of drinkers' legend. Then my food and a second pint arrived, and I smiled at Anne, my favourite server in The Hat, and set about putting behind me the world of airplanes, taxis, and clients. The first mouthful of my meal reaffirmed an ancient truth, that without regular doses of the best things that appeal to the flesh, life would be just a bad video game. Not that there are any good video games. The flavours of hops, malt, sausage, and a pile of mash smiling from beneath its crown of thick gravy were the best welcome home I could have imagined.

"Jim? Jim Cochrane? Is that you?"

For just a moment I imagined I was back at the speaker's podium, and a pudgy employee of the client (every client has at least one of these) was about to try to impale me on a tough question.

'No,' I said to myself. 'Nothing is going to divert me from enjoying this meal.'

"Jim?"

Looking around, I caught sight of someone roughly my age, blond hair several months on the shady side of a haircut, gazing at me intently, even hopefully.

"Buddy?" I said, the cerebral machinery having come up with a likely match. "Buddy Martin?"

Nods soon confirmed identities both ways, and I invited Buddy to bring his food to my table.

From my years of consulting work, I had picked up a thin smear of patience and diplomacy, although my boss intoned regularly, and ominously, that the smear would need to be a lot thicker if I wanted to play in the big leagues. A blast from my Coboconk past, in the form of Buddy Martin or under any other guise, was the last thing I expected, or wanted, but I put on a smile.

"I never believed I'd meet you here", Buddy said in what sounded like surprise and delight. "Do you live close by?"

I was tempted to say 'No', but then explained about my lovely pad, and we went through the usual 'How are you?' routines.

"Are you in Toronto now, Buddy?"

His nervous fidgeting told the story long before he articulated it.

"No", he said, interrupting himself to finish a last forkful of food and take a long swig from his pint. "No, I, ah, I'm in town for just a few days. I'm, ah, I'm looking for work."

"What do you do, Buddy?" I asked, then looked down to the task of finishing my own meal so as not to see him grope for an answer somewhere between naked truth and blatant falsehood.

I finished my bangers and mash, drained my second pint, then looked up and smiled at Buddy. He was still working on his answer.

"Another pint, Buddy?"

"Ah, no...I —"

"Go on!" I cajoled. "On me." And I waved at Anne and flashed a sign for two more.

Buddy smiled in relief and agreed.

"What do you do, Jim?" he asked, even though he hadn't answered the same question from me. Didn't matter. It was fairly clear that he was a labourer of some sort, probably a tradesman. Nothing wrong with that. Although it did seem to me that he must have known there would be a gulf between us. And so why identify himself? 'Be gracious, Cochrane', I said to myself. 'You're no hot shit'.

"I'm really just a glorified salesman", I said.

"But you're an engineer, aren't you?"

"Yeah, Buddy. But we all do basically the same sort of thing. We try to find work that needs to be done, we try to do it well, and we try to get along with people."

Our beer arrived, we raised glasses, smiled, and chugged.

"Have you been back to Coboconk lately?" he asked.

"No. Not since I left. I doubt that it's changed. And I expect there's nothing there for me any longer." I grabbed my beer and drank decisively, as if signaling the end of the matter. But there was something odd in Buddy's expression, so I followed up.

"Do you still live there?"

"No", he answered. "I'm in Lindsay now."

It seemed to me that a move like that would produce little change, just going from a very small puddle to a larger small puddle.

"And do you plan to move to Toronto?"

"No", Buddy said, shaking his head. "I got a couple of tips on jobs where I might be taken on. I plan, actually, to move back to Coboconk."

This was a surprise, and it seemed to me, suddenly, that there might be something I could learn from Buddy. So, I began questioning him.

As I expected, a number of people in my age cohort had stayed in the village, and had gone into things like real estate, handyman work, and plumbing. One had become the new village barber. But most of them had moved away. I knew of one other, the only person apart from me in my school year who had gone to university. She was now working for an insurance company. Buddy filled me in on the rest. Three had decamped to Lindsay, one to Peterborough, one to Kingston, and he had lost track of most of the rest.

"What will you do if, or when, you move back?" I asked.

His face brightened somewhat.

"Mrs. Weston wants me to become janitor and general handyman at the community centre."

Community centre, I thought. That's new.

"Why not go back right now?"

"Money has been a problem ever since amalgamation, since we became the City of Kawartha Lakes. Ridiculous, I think, but that's just the way things are."

"Why do you expect that to change? Why do you expect the purse strings will be loosened?"

"Ah!" he said, the tone of optimism in his voice being matched by his expression. "Our member on the council is really making waves. Looks like he runs circles around the mayor, who thought he had everything all sewn up. So, Mrs. Weston says just to be patient and to keep in touch."

"Who's the member?" I asked.

"Nat Thibodeau."

I knew there were Thibodeaus in Bobcaygeon but...

"Sounds like a lot of new people have moved in", I commented. There must have been a note of incredulity in my voice.

"Yes, indeed. In fact, if you went there today, you'd probably recognize only about a quarter of the people." Buddy nodded once, strongly, for emphasis.

Of course, I expected what he said was true.

We talked for another half-hour. By then it was past eleven o'clock, and he announced that he had to be getting on. We rose, shook hands, and he left. He didn't ask me for my address or any other contact information. I didn't ask him, not wanting to risk any embarrassment. I didn't expect to see him again.

But he did leave something behind. I didn't recognize it as such just then, but it was a low-level background conflict. When I examined things more closely about a month later, I realized that the door I had slammed shut on my Coboconk past was one I really didn't want to be opened again, but for no reasons that I could spell out.

Why?

Because it's past. It's gone.

Convenient. If it's gone, why are you still thinking about it?

Piss off. There's nothing there for me. I'm not going back.

But, in fact, I did.

II

It was more than six months later when the prod, the incentive, came to me in the mail. I wondered how they had got my address, but then remembered that I had signed up to a high school classmates site. Somebody must have passed on my information from there.

The prod was an invitation to a spring festival, to be held in the Coboconk community centre. I'm still not entirely sure why I decided to go. Curiosity? A chance to show off? Just some perverse primeval twinge?

The event was on a Saturday evening, and I drove there late in the day on Friday. It was a grey and cloudy afternoon. I don't know why I went straight to the village and had a two-minute look. My first impression was that the place was all too forlorn in its familiarity. A few sad, grey snowbank relics remained here and there, and that didn't make the first impact any less depressing. But the grass was returning and the buds on the trees were just about to pop. I had booked two nights in a small motel just south of the village, and I turned around and drove there. That night, I went into Fenelon Falls, had a decent meal, returned to the motel, and made an early night. On the morning of the festival, I took my time driving through the streets of Coboconk. Compared to the downer of the previous day, it was an eye-opener.

About half the houses had been spruced up to modern standards or demolished and replaced by new structures. I knew that the house I was raised in was no longer there, but I was shocked to see the tiny balsam sapling I had planted as a boy of ten. It was now more than forty feet tall. I realized that my shock wasn't at how much the tree had grown, but at being confronted by something small and quaint from my past that had transformed itself into a large and very different element of the present.

The car park at the community centre was as good a place as any, so I parked there, locked my car, and set out on foot. I had no specific expectations that I was aware of, but it was peculiar to feel that I might be about to become acquainted with a different face of my home village, and to have the sense that this process might yield a surprise or two. The basic physical features hadn't changed, of course. The streets were still the same, had the same names. And although I met at least twenty people as I walked, I recognized nobody. But there was a sense of things being different somehow.

I had lunch in what was once a tea room but now advertised itself as a bistro. Less than a day ago, I would have laughed at that change in name, considering it pretentious. But now it had a natural flavour — it was just another change that seemed somehow appropriate. After lunch, I drove to three neighbouring villages, places where once I had played ice hockey. I found that they had changed in a similar way.

Big deal, Cochrane. What did you expect? That you're the only one who's changed, moved forward? That everything else is static, frozen in dumb-ass hickdom?

But...

No, Cochrane. Don't go there either. Let's have none of this 'things haven't changed under the surface' shit. If you're not going to make an idiot of yourself tonight, you need a serious attitude adjustment.

I had brought a couple of books with me, half expecting to need to retreat to a more intelligent space, but now I realized that I needed a different sort of quiet time. I drove back to the motel and settled in with one of the books.

By five thirty, my mood had changed. The big shot, the small town boy made good, the asshole who had been lurking in the background, now had his eviction notice. I shaved, changed my shirt, and by six fifteen I was on my way back to the community centre.

To my surprise, there were four or five people I recognized, and they turned out to be not the inarticulate yokels that, to my shame, I seem to have expected. Interesting conversations ensued. Eventually I was introduced to Bruce Harris, and that's how I became involved in the project to save the old village railway station.

"Call me Bruce."

He was about sixty, had one of those happy, pinkish faces, curly steel-grey hair, a firm handshake, and a smile that was completely natural but one he had perfected through much use. But it was the eyes that caught one's attention: bright blue, clear, sparkling, and windows onto an active mind.

"I don't know your family name, although a few of the older people remember."

"No", I said. "We all moved away quite some time ago, and all within a couple of years."

"You didn't keep in touch with anyone here?"

"No. I imagine that's a common tale — for those who leave, that is."

We talked some more. I told him about our family home and some of the people I knew, and I gave him a few scraps about my post-Coboconk life.

"And what about you?" I asked. "I assume you're also an incomer. What brought you here?"

"I rented a cottage here for a couple of summers, liked the place, and just moved here."

"Simple as that?"

"Yes", he said. "As simple as that."

This reminded me how heavy, and how sticky, personal baggage can be, how it can tinge one's outlook permanently, and how one can evolve a completely different perspective if there is no baggage.

"What do you do here?" I asked.

"Oh, I'm retired. And before you begin wondering what a guy my age is doing being retired, let me just say there were some wise investments when I was younger. But I do have projects. The one that's keeping me occupied at the moment is the task of moving the old railway station."

"Moving it?"

"Yes", he said decisively. "If it stays where it is much longer, it's likely to have a slow, or maybe a fast, decline. We want to move it and repurpose it. We need a new medical centre. The local Chamber of Commerce has expressed interest in it as an office. But mostly we just don't want to let it have no function, to fall into decay and be demolished. And speaking of the station, it seems to me, from what you tell me of your background, that you're just the sort of guy we could really use on this project."

I smiled.

"I live more than a hundred miles away. I doubt that I could make any useful contribution."

"Not at all!" Harris said, brushing aside my hesitations. "But let's get something to eat. And I'd like to introduce you to a few people."

Well, suffice it to say, he did introduce me to a few people, and not surprisingly they were all familiar with the station project. It didn't take long for me to warm to the evening. And despite my earlier determination not to treat this visit as anything other than a one-off, arms-length trip to my home village, I found that I was warming considerably to the occasion and the company, and to the station project as well. The evening went by effortlessly. I mingled and talked, and even exchanged a few business cards, but I made no promises.

I had been back home in Toronto for a few days when a bulky envelope arrived in the mail, date-stamped the day after I left Coboconk. I set it down on my desk, next to the business cards that I had picked up from various people, including Harris. I hadn't touched the business cards, and I wasn't entirely sure I wanted to open the package, so I went about my day, eyeing it occasionally. After dinner, I decided I had delayed enough. I sat at my desk and opened the package. Inside was a full set of plans for the station move, along with a schedule, copies of various contracts, and a package related to the project's history. On top of those documents was a single slip of paper on which was written in a neat hand:

In case you're interested. Any thoughts or suggestions you might have would be received warmly.

Kind regards,

Harris

I began looking through the documents and was impressed right away at how much work had gone into this venture. As I read further, I pulled a pad toward me and began making some notes. After three hours, I had nine pages of notes. But I had also identified two areas where the planning could be beefed up, and I formulated two suggestions for rearranging tasks, suggestions that looked like they could save the project quite a few dollars. I typed my notes into a file on my computer, cleaned it up a bit, and saved it in a new directory that I called 'Coboconk Railway Station.' I then sent a short email to Harris listing my two suggestions using the email address on his business card. Having done this, I felt an odd sort of relief, a sense that I had now done something useful, made a couple of suggestions, and that was that.

Two days later, Thursday, at about eight o'clock in the evening, I received a telephone call from Harris.

It was a pleasure to meet and have some time to talk the previous weekend, he said.

Thanks very much for my suggestions. Most useful, he said.

He hoped that I had found the evening interesting, he said. Some others had mentioned that they enjoyed speaking to me.

He then made his pitch after a short pause.

"Could I interest you in another visit to Coboconk this weekend, Mr. Cochrane?"

"Well … it's really not all that convenient for me. Besides, I'm not at all sure…"

"I'll be straight with you, Mr. Cochrane. I really would like to pick your brains. You came up with two solid suggestions after having had only a very short time to look at the plans I sent you. I ask myself how much more you might be able to contribute if you were to … well … give it a bit more attention."

"Very well, Mr. Harris. I'll be straight with you as well. My work demands a great deal of me. I really cannot consider getting into another big project just now. I'm sure you understand."

"I do indeed, Mr. Cochrane, and in your shoes I probably would also be concerned. I don't want to try to drag you into anything. But I would like to ask for just eight hours of your time. That's all. After that, no further involvement."

Normally, I would see visions of scope creep before me, and when it comes to informal community projects like this one, the risks can be notorious. But for some reason, I was not disquieted at all. Maybe I believed him about the eight hours. He did seem to be a very pragmatic man.

I hedged.

But then I said yes, that I would come to Coboconk again.

III

Saturday morning, very early, I was on the road. At eight forty-five, I parked my car next to the Coboconk community centre, and sat thinking and sipping the coffee I had picked up on the way. The arrangement was that I would meet Harris at 9:30. We would have, I presumed, a day of discussions, I would then drive the few kilometres to the same motel I had used the previous weekend, and by noon on Sunday I would be back home. *Fin de l'histoire.*

At 9:15, I picked up the slim leather documents case containing the notes I had made earlier on the project, locked my car, deposited my empty coffee cup in the waste bin at the end of the car park, and entered the community centre. Voices came through the open door to a small conference room on the left.

There were five people, four men and a woman, seated at a table in the conference room. Harris was the only one of them I had met. Papers were spread out before them. I knocked and entered.

"Ah! Mr. Cochrane! Welcome! It's good to see you again! Please join us." And saying that, he handed me a folder of papers.

I was introduced to Des Richman, Trevor Penman, Eugene Wilson, and Nancy Thrush. Thrush was a retired school teacher. Richman had owned a small trucking operation. Penman was a land surveyor, recently retired, and Wilson was manager of the local Foodland store.

"We were just going through the list of upcoming tasks for the station project. Please! Take a seat."

I glanced down at the list of tasks and their descriptions on the sheets that had been handed to me. These contained more detail than the material that had been sent to me earlier, but it took less than five minutes to see where improvements could be made.

How to proceed? This was the primary question whenever it became clear that my contribution to a project might contain unwelcome news. I allowed the discussion to proceed, listening as the others worked their way transactionally through the tasks. I jotted a few notes on the pages in front of me, and drew my notes from earlier out of my documents case, half listening to the discussion.

"...and that will be the end of Phase 1", Harris said. "Phase 2 will be renovating the station at its new location."

He turned to me. "Any comments or observations, Mr. Cochrane?"

I set down my pen and looked around at them.

"Yes. A comment and then three suggestions. First, the comment. You have done an amazing job here. It's not just the initiative that's impressive. It's the fact that you've put together a very creditable plan. So, you should give yourselves a pat on the back."

I smiled and looked around at five nodding heads.

"And now my suggestions. Please don't be alarmed at what I'm about to say. I'll state my suggestions, then follow up with proposals on how these three items could be handled."

As I expected, there was a noticeable stiffening of expressions around the table.

I made my suggestions, then spent a few minutes on each of them, explaining what I thought should be done. When I finished, an ominous silence stretched out.

"Well!" Wilson said, a doubtful and unhappy expression on his face. "This comes as a considerable surprise." The hidden text was a sense of outrage that someone having no connection to the project and no background should suddenly turn up and poke holes in it.

Harris looked around the table before speaking.

"Let's look at this from a status quo point of view", he said, and then turned to me. "Suppose I suggested to you that one approach would be just to disregard your comments. What would be your response?"

I nodded and smiled.

"That's an entirely plausible reaction. Challenge the challenger. Here's what I would say in response. First, the project doesn't have what I would consider an adequately focused industrial safety strategy. Yes, I agree that you have a strategy, but I suggest that you beef it up a little. I say this for just one reason. If anything happened, an event involving personal injury, for example, there could be the possibility of exposure to legal and financial consequences. This is not by any means something that's difficult to remedy."

I looked at the five of them to gauge their reactions, and to show what I hoped was a positive and helpful face.

"Second, I suggest a slightly different emphasis on aspects of the new location, particularly on double-checking that the new foundations are adequate. I say this only because of the need to make triple sure there's no problem at the new site. Once again, this is a 'what if' situation. I'm not saying there's anything wrong, but it's better to be certain. Once again, easy to deal with since time is available."

Another sympathetic look around the table.

"Third, there are several tweaks that could be made to the overall management of the project. That, too, is easy to accommodate." And I outlined what I felt could be done and how it could be done.

I paused here once more.

"Please don't take any of this the wrong way. What you're doing here shows strong community spirit. It's competent and very admirable. But I think that this project should come off with zero hitches, and that there should be nothing for potential detractors to grab hold of."

"Detractors?" Thrush interjected. "We don't have any detractors!"

"Perhaps not", I responded. "But no physical operations have begun yet; the big bucks are still to be spent. I suggest that you should be trying to make sure that this project is as clean as a whistle — financially, technically, and politically. Under those circumstances there will be only winners, and you" — and here I indicated the five of them — "you will have something to brag about without any fear of contradiction."

The silence weighed heavily.

"Thank you", Harris said to me finally. He then turned to the others.

"My sense is that we can't ignore what Mr. Cochrane has said, even if it's not welcome news. Can we please discuss these points? I'll start."

The discussion went on for two hours. Thrush was the first to come round, Penman the last. They wanted to know what I felt my role in the project might be. At present, I told them, I had no role, but one could be defined.

At twelve thirty, I turned to Harris.

"If there's a place in town that will prepare and deliver sandwiches, allow me to treat you all to lunch."

A chorus of polite objections arose, but I persisted, and Harris eventually agreed. When we reconvened after lunch, the first genuine smiles made their appearances. I sketched out some details for changes, then walked them through what it all meant.

By four o'clock, I had broken every promise I had made to myself during the trip that morning from Toronto. I had become a full member of the station relocation team, and had committed time that I wasn't sure I had.

To my surprise, I felt good about all this, and even looked forward to it.

IV

It turned out that the changes made in response to my comments resulted in no drastic impacts on the schedule, and that in fact the increase in costs was more than offset by savings we found elsewhere. A lot of slack had been included in the schedule, fortunately, and all we did was reallocate that slack to those points where the uncertainties indicated that extra contingency was prudent.

I was now on a weekly schedule of trips to Coboconk, and at each meeting we went through the tasks again, checking and making sure. Few unforeseen problems arose, and those that did were all minor. Finally, there were three weeks to go before the big move. By that time, I had recalled the old station as I remembered it, but had also added a vast amount of new information and perspective because of having to do detailed physical checks linked to individual tasks. One set of these checks was to have an architect upgrade the old drawings we had unearthed for the station, confirming that the basic elements of the structure were as indicated and that the building retained its soundness and could withstand the strains that would be imposed by the move.

An inventory had been made of the relatively few items in the station that could have any historic value. Those that could be removed easily were packed up and put in temporary storage, presumably awaiting assessment by a curator. After several weeks of fairly close involvement in the project, I had spent a lot of time in and around the old station. Its present reality was now well known to me. But its past had also come back with some force. Walking through the rooms in the station yet again, it was easy to imagine the echoes from the high ceilings, the sounds of the telegraph key, the chatter that animated a full waiting room, the clipped conversation associated with ticket sales, and then the sound, far down the line, of a steam whistle as the train approached. There was a little bit of nostalgia involved, but it was more than that. Somewhere, somehow, I was undergoing an internal reconciliation between strong but probably distorted recollections and the here-and-now physical markers that had triggered my memory. I was somewhere between a long-gone blurry past and a hard-edged present that carried the enduring physical elements from that past. What I found most surprising was the discovery, within me, of a natural resistance to the whole station move, and when I examined it closely I could see that there was some sense of final uprooting. The rails were long gone, as were the storage sheds. The turntable and water station were gone. It was now just the old station sitting on some waste land. When the station was no longer there, that truly would be the end of the story, the last reminder stripped away. It was silly and juvenile, but I humoured myself by sitting amidst all these reminiscences.

Two days before the removal, I took a last walk through the station, still on the spot where it had sat for nearly a hundred years. Quite some time before I became involved, the last of the large removable items in the station — the station clock, an old Canadian National poster, the cast iron wall bracket on which the mail sacks had hung at one time — were unbolted from the walls and placed in a storage room in the community centre. When I had asked about any other items that might have been removed, I was told that Hector Duncan, a part of the project in its early days but now incapacitated by arthritis, had taken some things away and that they were now safely lodged in his basement. When I asked what these items were, nobody had a very clear idea.

Hector lived on the ground floor of a large two-storey house in the centre of the village. When he answered my knock on his door, I was faced by a solidly built man somewhere in his eighties, and although it was clear that he moved with difficulty, his open greeting and alert eyes signalled a mind that was not about to be restricted by an uncooperative body. I introduced myself, and he invited me in.

"Cochrane, eh? Yes, I remember your father, William. Remember you, too. You delivered our newspaper, but it would have been my wife had all the dealings with you then. Gone she is, these last eight years, before you ask."

He stumped through to his sitting room and offered me a seat.

"Coffee? Just made some."

I said yes, and immediately rose as he began hobbling to his kitchen.

"No. You stay here, young fellow. Everything in my kitchen is temperamental. Milk? Sugar?"

We sorted out the coffee agenda, and a few moments later we were seated and sipping. Hector's living room was a clean, tidy, and tasteful flashback to the 1970s, a situation maintained, I suspected, by the regular help of a cleaning lady. Against one wall was a bookcase containing titles that would do justice to any intelligent reader, and copies of two current newspapers and a bookmarked copy of *Middlemarch* were on the reading table next to Hector's seat.

"You said something about the station, as I remember, when we spoke. What can I do for you?"

I explained my late arrival role in the station project and my general interest in whatever he had removed from the station when it had been off-loaded by the railway.

"I'm interested in a general way, but would also like to have a list of the things that were placed in your safekeeping."

"Bit of a highfalutin term that, 'safekeeping'. I just wanted to keep all those things from being pinched, dumped, or broken up for firewood. Moved them all to my basement. Still there. Safe and dry. But I didn't keep any sort of inventory. You're welcome to take a look. I can't get down there any more, so I'll just have to tell you where it all is. I expect it will all have to come back up at some point."

We talked a bit more about the village, and his recollections of people who had once lived here. His body might have been going rusty, but there was nothing at all wrong with his mind. He could remember all sorts of things — how the arena had been declared unsafe and had to be knocked down, the replacement of the bridge over the river, and hearing the old-timers talk about the war, those who would talk about it.

"No", he said, in answer to my question. "Your father never said a word about what happened over there. He was — but I guess you know all about his condition when he returned."

I did. He was a broken man.

"But you don't want to waste your time listening to an old duffer. Let's get you downstairs so you can look at the things from the station."

He gave me detailed guidance on where to find the items from the station, and I went down the steep steps, into a basement that was dry and well lit. The air had that stale odour of an unventilated space, but when I got to the bottom of the stairs and looked around, it was a scene of neatness and order that met my gaze. Against one wall was a furnace, and next to it a woodworking bench, evidently not used for some time. On the adjoining wall were metal shelves, now empty, but what probably had held, at one time, jars of preserves, boxes of off-season clothes, and the general bits and pieces needed for handyman work.

Against the wall opposite the furnace, and held off the floor by three wooden pallets, were four items of various sizes, roughly crated and then wrapped in heavy plastic. Peering through the plastic and frames, I could make out what appeared to be the station master's chair, his desk, a pot-bellied stove, and a set of shelves that must have held tickets, railway notices, and all the other items that would have been involved in housekeeping for a small rural railway station.

The plastic had gone somewhat brittle, and it was an easy thing to open a couple of access holes through it so that I could get a closer look at the objects inside the crates. There was indeed the station master's chair and desk, and on the desk was the telegraph key and all the wiring and components that went with it. These were all neatly bundled together, and anchored to the surface of the desk by several loops of rope. Taking a closer look at the set of shelves, it looked as though there were still some very yellowed sheets, pads of paper, notices, and a somewhat dusty black book. Some sort of log kept by the station master? These items were all held in place by a single wrapping of plastic that covered all the open faces of the shelves.

I turned my attention to the desk. By reaching in through one of the holes I had made in the plastic wrap, I was able to open all but one of the desk drawers. The top drawer on the left side of the desk contained just a pair of shoes, looking very old and brittle. The drawer on the right had wooden file slots, within which were what looked like a whole series of 'orders of the day', or whatever they might have been called. The central drawer contained several nice-looking fountain pens, a half-dozen pencils, an ink bottle, two erasers, some loose papers, a set of keys, and a box made of wood inlay that looked very fine indeed. It was the only thing whose purpose was not evident, and my curiosity got the best of me. It was only just within reach. I lifted it from the drawer, drew it out through the hole in the plastic, blew a layer of fine dust from it, and opened it.

The box contained a medal, and it was a military honour.

V

I did something that I shouldn't have done.

I pocketed the box containing the medal and had no intention of telling Hector, or anyone else associated with the station project. At least, not just yet. In the small notebook I had brought with me, I jotted down a list of all the items I could see in the packages stored in Hector's basement. There were things here that belonged in a museum, and I wanted to make sure that the first step in this, making as comprehensive a list as I could, was completed.

Back in Hector's sitting room, I accepted the offer of another cup of coffee.

"I've made a list of the items from the station you have down there, Hector. Do you agree to me speaking to the station project people, probably Harris, and making some arrangements to have them brought up from your basement and handed over to a conservator?"

"Yes. Of course. That's why they're here, so they could be kept safe and intact, and put into professional hands eventually."

I asked Hector when he had transferred all these items.

"Oh! Long time ago! Must have been in the mid-sixties. Stu Dempsey, he was the last station master, he was very down about leaving the old station. He was already getting on. Nowhere else to go. The railway was closing lines and stations left and right. He stayed until they threw him out. That's when I moved all the stuff, right after he left."

Hector paused here, gazing into a past only he could see. "Dempsey moved to Lindsay, I think. I heard he died sometime in the eighties."

"Did you know him well?" I asked.

"No. Just to say hello to on the street and get together for the occasional drink. He was a railroader to the core. Never married, except maybe to the station itself. Kept that old station in first-class condition all the time. Must have broken his heart to leave."

"He must have had some friends here."

"Oh, he had friends", Hector said. "I considered him a friend. But in his personal life, I figure he was very solitary."

"Did Dempsey ask you to take care of this stuff?"

"No. But I helped him move his few personal things out of the station and into a small van when he left. It was all a huge rush, the railway wanting him out, wanting everything wrapped up as quickly as possible. He made two trips. At the end of the second trip he took one long last look at the station. Poor old bugger. It was then I decided I would move all those things out and stick them in my basement."

"Didn't the railway have something to say about that?"

Hector scoffed.

"They didn't care. The station, in fact the whole line, was just something they wanted to unload. The only thing they took was the small safe that sat in the station master's office. The rest they just abandoned."

Hector and I talked some more, then I thanked him and left, saying that either Harris or I would be in touch about retrieving the things from his basement.

"That's fine", Hector said, smiling. After a short pause, he added, "Don't be a stranger, young fellow. Drop by and see me again whenever you like."

We shook hands — a strong and, I thought, meaningful handshake on his part — and I left.

I had one more meeting with Harris, then I planned to head back to Toronto. I had some research to do and a growing curiosity to quench. The meeting with Harris was collegial. He had reconsidered his impatience at my insisting on reviewing things again and again, when I pointed out how many items those reviews had turned up, items which hinted at sleeper problems. None of these problems was a showstopper, but any one of them would have been a real headache if it hadn't been unmasked early. On this occasion, our walk through the upcoming tasks found nothing. I was back home by six o'clock that evening.

Sitting at my desk, I opened the wooden case and stared at the medal for several minutes. It was clear that it had been protected from the effects of damp and pests. The metal was bright and fresh, and the ribbon was almost pristine. It took me only a few minutes of searching to learn that what lay before me was a Military Cross with one bar, that this was an award created in 1914, and that only about three hundred Canadians had been given this honour. Another hour of online searching yielded the names of those recipients, and the fact that one of them had come from the village of Norland, about seven or eight kilometres north of Coboconk. Of course, there was no reason that the medal I had come across had necessarily belonged to that gentleman, whose name had been given as Arthur Michael Tolman, but I had to start somewhere.

In fact, I had decided to approach the matter from two directions. First, I would find out as much as I could on my own. Only then would I reveal to Harris what I had come across, and turn the medal over to a competent authority.

My searching began yielding results almost immediately. Arthur Tolman had been born in Norland on June 12, 1896, and had died on April 4, 1969. After some digging, I found a short obituary stating that he had served during World War I (service and location not given), that he had worked as a mechanic in Toronto, then as a carpenter in Bracebridge, and that at his death he was living on his small farm near Victoria Road. There were no further details.

Another two hours of digging failed to turn up any information on a wife or any children. There were other avenues to pursue, but at that moment I was running out of time. It was getting late, and the next day promised intense work on a number of consulting projects, so I couldn't sit up all night. I made notes on where I could be looking next, filed a dozen or so electronic documents, put paperwork away in a folder, locked the little wooden box in my desk, and retired.

The week flew by. Long days, and nights spent planning the next day's work left no time each evening for anything other than a meal and bed. But then things relented on Friday, and that evening I found a few hours to get back into the story on Arthur Tolman. Against my expectations, I found a grave, and was also able to locate his death certificate. The cause of death was given as "exposure". I embarked on a much larger search of small newspapers for the year of his death. It took a long time, but by ten forty-five that evening, I had located a small note in the obscure local newspaper *The Victoria County Register*, a tiny publication that served various villages in Victoria County. One of those villages was Victoria Road.

The article reported the following:

"On April 5, Arthur Tolman was found dead in his home just off Blanchard's Road. He was due to meet a friend, William Aire, that morning, and when Mr. Tolman failed to appear Mr. Aire checked his home and alerted the authorities. Police reported that all the windows in Mr. Tolman's house were open, despite the chilly temperatures, and Mr. Tolman was found on his bed. Mr. Tolman was 72 years old. He had farmed his small holding for eight years. He had no wife or family."

I thought about this for some time. What had happened? Tolman had survived for fifty years following the Great War. His body had been found by a friend. He had been an old man who met death alone. How had he died? Death by exposure in one's own home seemed very strange. Had there been foul play? And if so why? And how?

Sad. Odd.

But at this distance in time, more than forty-five years later, what could I hope to learn, to supplement the few meagre threads already known? Indeed, what prospect was there that anything further might be found that was related to the medal?

The medal.

I had already resolved to make the offer to move the items stored in Hector's basement, place them in the community centre, and take the lead on identifying a conservator who could come and provide advice on what should be done next. In the process of moving those items, it was my plan to have the existence of the medal 'come to light'. What this meant was that I could judge how much time to block off before I needed to declare the discovery of the medal, and, inevitably, hand it over also to the conservator.

Time to decide, I thought. So, I decided.

I booked a week of leave, starting the following Tuesday, since there were things to do on Monday at work that couldn't wait.

Tuesday rolled around, and by then I had a good picture of what needed to be done. The entire day was spent on searching veterans' records online in various locations. Very little came out of that, except the information that Arthur Tolman had been born to Rebecca and Samuel Tolman. A bit more digging revealed that Samuel Tolman had died on November 6, 1946, and Rebecca had died on February 22, 1951. There seemed to be no other information on either of them, and that branch of my trail came to an end there.

Two other possible leads could be followed, and some of that work would be done while I was in Coboconk. But right away I began looking for information on William Aire. After a lot of digging, I found that he had died in the hospital in Lindsay on August 8, 1976. He had also lived in Victoria Road, not far from Tolman's place. It looked like some poking around in Victoria Road was in order.

Having done all that and printed what I would need, I retired for the night, ready for an early start the next day, Wednesday, making Coboconk my base but beginning to inquire right away in Victoria Road.

I awoke early next morning and a question sat sullenly in my mind.

'What are you doing, Cochrane, wasting an insane amount of time on an old medal?'

For once, I decided to humour this awkward inner voice.

'It wasn't all that long ago that you were moaning about my aversion to having anything to do with Coboconk. Now that I've spent time in Coboconk, and become interested in something as a result, you're moaning again. What gives?'

'What gives is your sense of proportion. Or lack of one. It's fine to take an interest in something, but this is turning into a major project.'

'And this is of concern to you — why?'

'One of us has to keep things between the fences.'

'You know what you are? You're a shit disturber, and purely to generate olfactory offence.'

'Well, if you want to be —'

'I'm tuning out. You aren't interested in anything positive. Goodbye.'

At that point, I jumped out of bed wearing a smile, happy to have begun the day on a clear victory.

Looking back, it was about then that things began to speed up.

VI

The two threads I planned to follow were, first, to try to find anyone who knew anything about either Arthur Tolman or William Aire, and second, to try to find any trace of Stu Dempsey. Both were long shots, but at the very least those possibilities had to be exhausted.

A long day spent asking various people in Victoria Road about Tolman and Aire yielded faint nibbles, but nothing resembling a bite. Two people knew the names, and knew from older relatives no longer around where both men had lived. Inquiries of the current owners of the properties drew complete blanks. This was nothing more than I expected.

I then went back to Hector Duncan's place. He welcomed me as enthusiastically and generously as on the previous visit.

Over coffee once again, I began asking about Dempsey. Hector related general information from memory, including dates and wisps of conversation with Dempsey that he could recall, but nothing more. He knew that Stu Dempsey had a brother named Graham, and that Graham had lived in Lindsay.

"That's as much as I know", Hector said finally. "I think Stu went to live with his brother in Lindsay initially, after he left Coboconk that is. Stu and I talked every now and then when he lived here, but we had no real reason to stay in touch after he went off to Lindsay."

We talked a bit more.

"Victoria Road?" Hector said, in some surprise. "Well, yes, he did know the station master there, but he never mentioned anyone else."

I probed further.

"Tolman? No. I don't remember Stu ever mentioning someone of that name. Lived in Victoria Road, did he?"

Another probe.

"His name? Well, I think it was … let me see … Archer? No, not Archer. Barber?…Ah! Barker! It was Barker! Don't recall a first name. Probably I never knew it. Yes. Stu did talk a little about Barker as station master in Victoria Road."

We chatted a bit more, and then I left. Two more razor-thin leads to follow.

Back in Victoria Road, I discovered that Leslie Barker had died early in the seventies, having been pensioned off by the railway. He had a son who had moved back to Victoria Road following a career in Toronto, but the son could tell me nothing about either Stu Dempsey or Arthur Tolman.

"The names ring a distant bell, but that's all."

In Lindsay, I tracked down Graham Dempsey's daughter, a Mrs. Angela Travers, who lived there in a well-kept house on Bond Street. My consulting experience helped me overcome her initial look of suspicion, projected at me through a partially opened door. A business card, indicating that I wasn't about to try to flog something she didn't want, got me inside her house. Once I had explained about the station in Coboconk, her reserve melted and she became more forthcoming. I chattered on about the station in Coboconk, the reason for moving it, the upcoming move itself, and my own boyhood Casey Jones dreams. She began to smile.

"Yes. I remember Uncle Stu quite well", she said, in answer to my question. "He and my father became close after Uncle Stu moved to Lindsay, so I saw a lot of him. A very kindly and gentle man."

"Did he ever show you anything from his time as station master in Coboconk?"

"Eventually", she said. "Yes. But it took some time for him to overcome the bitterness he felt at being dumped by the railway. He wanted to stay on at the station in Coboconk, live there in retirement, but they wouldn't allow that. It all seemed very mean-spirited of them, because after Uncle Stu left, they just closed down the station and abandoned it. I think he made an offer on it to the railway about a year after he left, but they just told him the matter was closed."

"Did he have any records, pictures, memorabilia from that time?" I asked, having no real expectations.

"In fact, he had quite a large file of stuff. He left it to my father, and it passed to me when my father died."

"Do you still have it?" I asked, trying not to seem too eager.

"Yes, but I haven't looked at it for years."

"Is there any possibility I could see it?"

"Well ... I don't know ... it's all personal family stuff", she said, before a long pause. "Oh, why not. They're all gone now. Just give me a few minutes." And she went off to another room. To my surprise she returned carrying a largish banker's box.

"I organized it all some time back. There are family photos, some personal correspondence, and a file of documents from Uncle

Stu's working past. I'm assuming that that file likely will be of most interest to you."

That sounded like a conditional offer, not particularly open to negotiation, so I nodded and smiled. She pulled a folder from the box and looked in it for a few moments before passing it over to me.

The file contained about forty or fifty items. There were about ten pages of official communication with the railway. There was a citation from the village of Coboconk recognizing how well the station was maintained and how much that was appreciated by the people in the village. There were a half-dozen newspaper clippings, now brown and becoming very brittle. There was an announcement of the upcoming closure of the station and the entire railway line, the text angrily annotated presumably by Stu Dempsey. And then there were four letters, the last one dated June 1954. I scanned them quickly, stopped, and held my breath.

In the letter bearing the latest date, after the "Dear Stu", and after a couple of paragraphs that sounded like local news of interest at the time, the letter continued:

"This brings me to the package I gave you last week when I visited Coboconk. I would like you to keep it for me. I didn't deserve it, and I no longer want it. It was your uncle Edward who really deserved it. I see his face always now, and the faces of so many others I was with in that God-forsaken mud hole. Please look after it for me, for your uncle's sake."

The letter then carried on with other bits of news. Turning to the end of the letter, I noted the signature: 'Arthur'. It seemed that I had struck oil.

"Did you have another uncle?" I asked Mrs. Travers.

"No. But I did have a great uncle. Uncle Edward. I never met him. He was killed in the First War."

I was thinking how I might ask to have this material copied, when she completed her previous statement.

"At Vimy Ridge."

As it does with many people, the name 'Vimy Ridge' has great power to resonate at many levels, and it did then with me. For several moments, I was stuck in some distant space.

"Will you want to make a copy of these letters?" she asked.

"May I?" I responded, almost in disbelief.

"Yes. It sounds like these letters are related to something important. If they can fill some gap in what you're working on, then that must be done. What those young men were put through back then was just...". She shook her head, still unable to fathom what had happened almost a century earlier.

"Perhaps I can take them down to the public library..."

"No need for that", she said. "I'm a bookkeeper, operate my own small business. I can make copies here on my printer. Let me do that now."

I handed the file over to her and she went off to another room. I could hear the sound of a printer, and she soon returned and handed me the copies.

We talked a little longer. She asked what the connection was that brought me to her place. I told her that the letters were almost certainly from another young man who had served in World War I, but that there were some things we wanted to authenticate.

"When the station is moved, it will be relocated near the Legion in Coboconk. If we are able to nail down everything, these letters will be of great interest."

"I can see that", she said, then nodded and smiled.

She looked around suddenly as if something important had been missed.

"I'm a very poor hostess. I'm sorry. I should have offered you a cup of something. Would you like one before you leave?"

"A cup of tea would be very welcome. Thank you."

Twenty minutes later, we had shared a small pot of tea, and I thanked her once more for everything, promising to keep her informed on whatever we found. At that point, she reached into a pocket of her sweater and pulled out a business card. We said a pleasant goodbye, she closed her door, and I moved toward my car as quickly as I could.

Over the course of the next week, I juggled consulting work and railway station work. In the evenings I was putting in long hours trying to nail down details. The picture emerged slowly.

Arthur Tolman and Edward Dempsey had both served in the 38th Battalion at Vimy Ridge. Edward Dempsey was killed on April 9, 1917. Arthur Tolman survived Vimy Ridge and the war, and I was able to confirm that he was awarded a Military Cross with one bar. But no matter where I searched, or how diligently I searched, I could find nothing that would link the medal I had found in Stu Dempsey's desk to Arthur Tolman. There was the letter to Stu Dempsey signed "Arthur" and referring to "the package I gave you". Was that the medal? It was reasonable and plausible to assume so, and that the medal had been Tolman's medal. Had it been Tolman's hope to give away the medal, and to see his ghosts go with it? Survivor guilt was a powerful force among the troops who returned home. The fighting men and boys over there had been in a fearsome crucible, where the bonds formed were far stronger than anything experienced in civilian life. The human cost among survivors was enormous. PTSD was unknown then by that name. The behaviour of men afflicted by it was all too often branded 'cowardice'. The number of suicides is unknown. The amount of suffering over the years must have been collosal.

It seemed clear enough that I had all the material I was ever going to get. Based on that, I drew what conclusions I could.

The medal most likely had belonged to Tolman.

Tolman and Edward Dempsey almost certainly had fought side by side.

Tolman had travelled to Coboconk in the 1950s and had given his medal to Stu Dempsey.

There was probably no foul play involved in Tolman's death. His ghosts did not go with the medal. They stayed with him. And in the end he escaped them in the only way left open to him.

Three days after the station move had been completed and our small private celebration of that event was over, I organized the recovery of the items from Hector Duncan's basement, "found" the medal, and a bit less than a week after that I turned it over to Harris, along with the folder giving the results of my research.

There were questions, and I either answered them honestly or passed off some plausible responses. From there, the matter was taken up by serious professional military researchers, but they found nothing more than I had turned up, apart from a few unimportant details: a full set of dates concerning Arthur Tolman's medal, and details of his demob and return to Canada.

After returning home from France, Tolman had lived in quiet obscurity, saying nothing about his war or his honour. Now, almost a hundred years after the fact, he was recognized.

It was a Saturday afternoon, and I stood with Harris in the community centre car park, getting ready to return to Toronto. We had both spent a good deal of time working on the tasteful display now occupying a prominent place in the Legion, something to honour Arthur Tolman and his fallen companion, Edward Dempsey. I looked toward where the old railway station had been, where I had come so many times as a boy on my bicycle. I also looked out over Coboconk. It was bathed in afternoon sun. The houses were scattered in ordered semi-confusion over the undulating land on the other side of the Gull River. It was the same, yet it wasn't the same. Years ago, it had been a place that I couldn't wait to leave. But now…?

I smiled at Harris. We shook hands. I climbed into my car and drove south.

All this business had thrown up images, and they paraded before me now, images of times long gone, of friends lost, and of new friends found.

"Lost Friends" is a fictional account of a real event. In 1995, the old railway station in Coboconk was indeed moved from the spot where it had sat for almost a century to a new location in Laidlaw Heritage Village. But all the characters in "Lost Friends" are entirely fictional.

In addition, the actual relocation of the station was an outstanding example of community spirit and excellence of execution. In that real event, the problems depicted in "Lost Friends" simply did not exist.

Discovering Jericho

It was the first time I was conscious of hearing wood pigeons. Oh, I probably had heard them during my previous two months on the Continent, but it was here, waking early in my digs, looking out the window at the brilliant blue sky, that I first became aware of that rather tedious four-note cadence, a musical lick that more often than not ended irrationally after Note One. I awoke, heard the sound, then awoke again, perhaps a half-hour later, to the patter of light rain on my window.

My digs on Walton Crescent consisted of a room in a rooming house that was better than average for the time. But the place acquired real standing once I learned, within a day or two of moving in, that I was in that part of Oxford called Jericho. I took great delight in this. I walked the streets of Jericho, all of them, right down to the canal.

"Jericho? Why Jericho?"

Explanations were offered. They seemed plausible, easy inventions moulded around the facts. The comment by the old barman in the *Jericho Tavern* seemed closest to the mark.

"Mists of time. Nobody really knows where the name came from. Another pint, sir?"

But that was a long time ago. Now on another return visit, my first time back on Walton Crescent, I find the house still there. No surprise, of course. The landlady is long gone, but no surprise there either. And things are definitely spiffed up compared to what I remember. But then memory is…

My first stay in Oxford, back then, was while I was approaching the end of my course at university. At the time, I was preparing for what became a rewarding and challenging career. Now here I am again, back in Oxford, placing the other metaphorical career bookend on the shelf. My first week or so in Oxford all those years ago was exciting, and the reason for that, I have concluded, was that I learned so much in such a short time. Being in one place, rather than flitting around like a tourist, caused me to interact with many things and people, and those interactions quickly revealed how little I had learned about the world in my first twenty years. Not only was Oxford different from anything I knew, it reflected a breadth and depth I hadn't even suspected. History was all around me, and not just in monuments, marker plaques, and physical structures. The way people dressed, the whole social scene, the pubs, street names, the buildings projecting different past realities but now huddled together today, the quality of some of the newspapers, the ways people used the language, the full range of sardonic, ironic, caustic, deadpan, and other expressions, these all hit me with the force of an express train. "Dreaming spires" suddenly became a kind of ineffable reality, something more than an advertising slogan, or a Pavlovian linguistic bite offered in reflex on hearing the syllables 'ox' and 'ford'.

And then the years piled up like self-stacking cord wood. Since that first stay, I have read almost all the novels set in Oxford, pored through guidebooks, and studied many maps of the city, some dating back to the eighteenth century. I guess I was just saving my return to Jericho until now, my significant but long-delayed return visit to Oxford. Naturally, I've seen all the episodes of the television series *Morse*, *Endeavour*, and *Lewis*, and have read, multiple times, the books by Colin Dexter. They provide one view, easy to absorb.

But I've noticed that during those cord-wood decades it seems that I had lost something. Lost it? Never had it? At first I was just aware that some undefined element was missing. There was a lacuna. The realization came to me as I walked through the streets of Oxford, past the spot where Latimer, Ridley, and Cranmer, high-ranking Protestants tried for heresy, were burnt at the stake in 1555 and 1556, past The Eagle and Child — well, not really past it since I stopped there for a drink — past the building that back then had housed my local watering hole, The Horse and Jockey. A once and future pub? And eventually I completed my path of exploration, that included some delightful meandering. Of the things I wanted to see again, I kept the best until last. I prowled in Waterstones (formerly Dillons) for an hour, strolled along Broad Street, then drooled in Blackwell's for an hour and a half, ending up in the White Horse where I leafed through the four purchases that were the result of that almost four hours of labour. And in both Waterstones and Blackwell's, choosing is indeed labour, the alternative being a great tonnage of bibliographic freight, and bankruptcy.

A good pint is often a source of inspiration, and that was the case once again in the White Horse. The nature of my lacuna, a general awareness that had grown over time, came into sharper focus. I had spent too much time, too many years, tied to engineering drawings, thermodynamic calculations, and seemingly endless disputations about tolerances. I had lost contact with something of great importance: that essential complement to the tunnel-vision exactitude of our modern world. And what is that component? Well, it's the gentle power flowing from a life suffused by literature, epistemological ponderings, and attention to the inherent contradictions and partial clarity of history. I won't say that I had that feeling way back then, when I was in Oxford. I was far too green and untried then. I hadn't yet learned the delights of a nimble-footed two-step through that forest of things intellectual. Nor had I been arm-wrestled into accepting that the tedious demands imposed by the world had to be met, demands to be complete and correct in each element of that great flood of life's trivialities. Perhaps it was best, back then, to have been in my state of unquestioning acceptance, ready to believe most things I came across, since it was all new.

It's easier to construct defences and justifications after the fact. And in a physical world so dominated by technology, there are many who will welcome technology's critics and sceptics, especially if they are, like me, delinquents from the flock. You see, I entered the working world as a card-carrying techie, proudly waving my engineering degree. But then I toppled sideways into heresy, began reciting poetry, was even caught one day reading Dostoyevsky instead of scribbling equations on the whiteboard next to the coffee machine. Now, I know that there are people out there who will rise up indignantly, waving tracts by C. P. Snow and other worthies, coming to my defence, and insisting that the arts world has standards just as demanding as those in science and engineering. In both realms, there is the same struggle to reconcile exactitude and ignorance, to extract clarity from uncertainty. All true. Except for the failure to acknowledge the bequest to us by Newton and Laplace of a very different outlook, one that turned out to be a crippling constraint. That bequest is a view of the world as a vast interplay of metaphorical billiard balls. That worldview has delivered handsomely in some ways. There is no doubt that it has given us understanding and control of the physical world, beyond anything its creators might have imagined. It has helped us mould the physical world practically at will, producing things that work well, delivering the means to health, education, and a rich source of intellectual fulfillment. The promise indeed was almost limitless. But those same metaphors have also blinkered us, and by focusing so strongly on only those aspects of the world we see as 'physical', they have left us impoverished in other ways.

Back again in Oxford, I felt that I could pick up the threads from that earlier time, peer once more through an unblemished, diaphanous veil of youth. It's still just the same Oxford, after all. And I found that to be true. The presence of the place is overwhelming. Its buildings, structures, atmosphere, have acquired that sanctity conferred by age and use. It has accreted deep sediments of meaning. Oxford back then had taken me by the hand, showed me what could be done through an immersion in the arts, framed an outlook that I should build upon. Oxford was now chastising me, it seemed, for backsliding, for just not trying during so many intervening years.

But there is something about observer and observed. Not everyone sees a thing the same way, and I had heard, over the years, so many accounts that I couldn't square with the Oxford I was sure I knew. But then, I worked it out. There are plenty of people who spend a few days in Oxford, claim bragging rights of some sort, and then leave, wondering secretly what all the fuss is about. Having a reason to stay there for quite a few weeks, I was forced to look more deeply.

My sense of Oxford was built up gradually, during that time almost forty years ago. I remember early morning light in August making the soft stone of New College glow proudly. I remember a pre-dawn walk on a Saturday that took me to Boar's Hill, and looking back I saw a thick covering of mist pierced by the tips of many college spires that caught the sun. I recall walking in the now long gone orchards at Rowstock Corners and having a powerful sense of the colour and aroma associated with ripening cherries. And there was that emblem of modernity, the Didcot Power Station (still under construction at the time), appearing to float poetically on a raft of low cloud, only to chug out a vast amount of rather less poetic waste after the energy and matter in the coal it burned had been separated.

The White Horse was my favourite pub back then, and I smiled to see that it still revelled in its usual delightful congestion. Someone nudged my chair as they passed behind me. There was a nice countercurrent diffusion of empty glasses toward the bar and fullies away from it. I gazed in perplexity at my pint and its own entropic decline, and pondered our tenuous grip on both beer and time. I was pleased just to be here again, and expected nothing more than atmosphere. An energetic exchange of greetings caused me to look up, but my panoramic view of the bar was suddenly blocked by the image of a pair of jeans straining to contain their heavy-set owner. The wearer slid sideways onto his seat, restoring my line of sight to a largish framed picture of John Thaw. Here at the White Horse is where quite a few scenes from *Morse* episodes were shot. My first pint, now nearing extinction, had done its job, had shoved the Toronto reality of yesterday off into the wings. The second pint, my Oxford welcome, was always the best, and seeing a lull at the bar, I sprinted for a refill.

Back at my table, I began looking through my catch from Waterstones, but lingered over one volume in particular, a copy of *The Moving Toyshop*, which would replace the copy that, at some point, went missing from my shelves. I flicked through it lovingly.

"Nicely written. But a bit dated now."

I raised my head to find the source of this assessment, which turned out to be a balding but fully alert gent at the next table over. He wore a well broken-in Harris tweed jacket, a pale-green cotton shirt, and what seemed to be a knitted homespun tie, and what was left of his hair retained most of its original sandy-brown colour. He regarded me through washed-out blue eyes which displayed nevertheless the intensity of one possessing boundless curiosity.

"One could say that about Oxford itself", I countered.

He beamed a delighted smile, raised his glass, and nodded his head in a manner that seemed to say 'a palpable hit'. We drank.

"I like the way Crispin talks about rural Oxfordshire and about Aylesbury", I said. "It might refer to a long bygone time, but I think we've lost it to our cost."

Here we were, two old boys who didn't even know each other's names, and now he regarded me with renewed scrutiny.

"You speak knowledgeably about Oxford, apparently, but in an accent that isn't consistent with that knowledge. Were you a student here, sir?"

"Not at the university, no. But anyone who visits this city for more than a day or two, and is worth his salt, must be a student of Oxford."

Having uttered that rather poncy statement, I gestured for him to join me, which he did.

"David Smollett", he said offering his hand after ensuring that his pint had made a safe landing.

"Charles Kent", I said, smiling at him and not expecting any juvenile quips involving Clark's brother. There weren't any.

"Where are you from, Charles, and how long are you stopping in Oxford?"

"Toronto. I'll be here four days."

"So", he said, and there was a very slight downturn to one corner of his mouth. "Not long."

"Long enough", I replied. "Old haunts."

We drank another half window each.

"Retired?" he asked.

"Yes. Six months ago, from engineering. You?"

"Yes. From the water board. Seven years ago. My wife died three years back, but at least we had four years almost continuously together."

"Oh. I'm sorry to hear that."

"Yes. Well. The way of the world. I've adjusted to it. Won't ever really get over it I expect."

He shifted abruptly in his chair, and smiled suddenly.

"I spent three years in Toronto."

"Oh, yes?"

"Yes. Back in my Bohemian days. Seems odd for someone from Europe to spend a Bohemian period in Toronto. It was 1967. Yorkville. The whole Gordie Lightfoot thing. I was lead guitar in a band called Long Black Hare. We were quite good. But then I woke up one morning and wanted something different. Did an Arthur Rimbaud."

"And then Oxford?"

"Yes. By a long route."

"Have you been back to Toronto?"

"No. It was such a distinctive time. Going back would just ruin it."

We talked more. I bought us two more pints. He asked about my interest in Oxford, and I told him of my discovery of Jericho, the walk to Godstow lock, being on the trail of The Inklings, Tolkien and his literary group.

That seemed to pique his interest, and I got him talking about himself. About being one of a group of male friends who called themselves the Door Knockers, for instance.

"Good fun. Six of us. We do a cyclic tour of Oxford pubs. We visit only the good ones, but even then it takes weeks to get to all of them."

"And then you start over?"

"Yes. Sounds daft, doesn't it?"

"No. Not at all. I could easily imagine myself doing that."

"Well, then. Move to Oxford, Charles. I'll put your name forward."

I had to smile at his irresistible twinkle. Couldn't help it.

And he belonged also to something called The Route Canal, a group of men and women who did canal walks. I asked him about that and he talked freely about some of their recent walks. As he spoke, I observed him. Life had evidently knocked him about somewhat, given him a few liver spots, stolen his soulmate, but hadn't put even a dent in what seemed to be an unquenchable zest for life.

He asked me about my life in Toronto.

I told him about my wife Teresa. He face registered immediate and touching concern.

"Yes, it was painful, but not nasty. It was just something that had run its course, we both recognized that. As divorces go, it was simple and straightforward. We stay in touch as friends."

And I talked about our son Victor, that apple of all four of our eyes. Successful. Well-adjusted. A civilized and compassionate human being.

As the levels in our pints drifted down toward 'Empty' it occurred to me that we were both gazing through windows. Were we both basically inside looking out, out from our world to another world, a world outside? Or were we really outside looking in? Or was it different for each of us?

Here was my new acquaintance, David, quite clearly seeing 1960s Toronto in his mind, a world that no longer exists, and I suppose that he was right not to go back just for a painful confirmation of that non-existence. But then there was me, here in an Oxford that was physically very similar after so many years. Details are different, of course, and the person I was then no longer exists. But I could come here again, now, and lay down another layer of recollection using the physical Oxford of today. In fact, that was exactly what I was doing.

"You had digs back then, when you were here earlier?" David asked.

"Yes", I said eventually, caught somewhat off guard. "In Walton Crescent. I became fascinated by the notion of living in a place called Jericho. But the more one knows, the easier it is to assess and assimilate new information. I've learned more about Jericho since then, so I wanted to come back and look again more closely."

We drained our glasses. I looked at David inquiringly.

"No more for me, thank you", he said, interpreting my gaze correctly. "But I usually go for a bit of a ramble on my way home. Would you care to accompany me?"

"Very much so. Yes please."

"Then let's be off."

We strolled back along Broad Street, crossed Cornmarket, then carried on along George Street.

There were fewer people about here. It was a warm humid evening, the shops were now closed, and the sky seemed to be clinging to that long, faint, northern twilight.

A light, misty rain began to fall. Fuzzy halos formed around the streetlights. I mentioned to David that I recalled nights like this, that I found them soothing, atmospheric.

"I've always enjoyed this sort of English weather", he said, in a way that made me feel as though he was speaking to a compatriot. I suppose because of my connection to Oxford I did feel like that, certainly wanted to feel like that.

We walked on, and I had lost all track of where we were.

"Where are you staying, Charles?"

"Not far", I said, "at a B&B called The Clarendon."

"Yes. I know it. I live about ten minutes further along, up the Banbury Road. I'll drop you off at your B&B on my way past. But not just yet. I'm finding this very pleasant."

I hoped that my smile told all, signalled my complete agreement.

Suddenly, I knew that we were in Walton Crescent. We passed by my old digs, but I didn't mention that to David. It was as much his walk as mine, moreso even, and I was just along for the ride.

We moved from street to street. Soon I had no idea once again where I was, and that seemed perfectly fine. The terrace houses on either side were dark and silent. The misty rain continued. A murky light still tinged the sky.

The sounds of traffic, quite prominent earlier, had now faded. The street felt uneven under my feet. Cobbles? Somewhere to my left, I heard someone cough. A cat cried, wanting to be let in. Apart from that there were just the muted sounds of our syncopated treads. We passed through a cloud of something. Smelled like coal smoke. Impossible, I thought. Today? But that was one of the nice things about quite a few spots in Europe. Many different times seem to coexist, in a way that is entirely natural. Timeless, almost.

To my left, the light showing through a window seemed rather pale and a bit flickery. Looking in, I saw two people sitting at a table, a candle between them. And up on the wall, was that a gas lamp?

We walked on, and I was suddenly aware that there were no cars parked in the street.

Then, in the distance, I could have sworn I heard the sound of a horse, walking slowly…

Fool's Cap

My brother and I have quite a history. One of the first things I remember about him is that we got along fairly well once I learned not to touch him and that he didn't like anybody seeing him pee.

One day not too long after I learned these things, I was looking for him. I had looked through most of our house. "Where's Mikey?" I asked my mother, who was folding clothes on the dresser that sat at the end of the upstairs hallway, an odd place to be doing that.

"He's peeing." That was perhaps my earliest clear memory of Mikey and privacy. The door to the bathroom was closed. I knew she was waiting for him to finish; then she would go into the bathroom and help him pull up his pants and tuck in his shirt.

Mikey didn't mind our mother seeing his 'thing', he just couldn't stand anybody having a line of sight to him when he was peeing, not even when he was sitting down. It was just one of Mikey's odd but endearing traits.

Mikey was three and I was five when we became friends. That was in addition to being brothers. Being friends meant doing stuff together, like counting the marbles I kept in the drawstring cloth bag my mother made to contain them and rearranging the Monopoly money. The play money had to be laid out according to colour in very neat piles, all the notes facing the same way, and all the edges lined up perfectly. Mikey wouldn't let me put the game away until we had done that. From the time we became friends, Mikey got used to the idea of us sleeping in the same room. Our mother was concerned, but it was more fun that way. The only condition was that it couldn't be in the same bed because of the risk that I might roll against him. If that happened he would start shouting.

Being friends also meant comparing 'things'. We didn't do this very often, but there seemed to be something exciting about going into our room, closing the door, and pulling down our pants and underwear. Then we looked at each other's 'things'.

"Will it get any bigger?" Mikey asked.

"I don't know", I said. "Maybe."

"Have you seen Mommy's 'thing'?"

"No", I said, and then wondered why I hadn't.

"Have you seen Daddy's 'thing'?"

"Yes. When he was peeing. Last week."

"Does he pee every week?" Mikey asked.

"Yes", I said. This was a problem I could work out. I pee every day, I thought, so Daddy must pee at least every week.

That was all a long time ago. Now Mikey and I are both in our fifties.

I still visit Mikey every couple of days, in his room in the sheltered accommodation about two blocks away from where Linda and I live. Mikey comes to our place for dinner once a month, and he's happy doing that now that our two children, Maria and Annie, have grown up and moved out. While they lived at home, they made Mikey feel uncomfortable. But he likes Linda and he's happy to have dinner with us on the third Wednesday of each month. Dinner that evening is always meatloaf with peas and carrots and a butter tart for desert. That's all that Mikey will eat at our place.

Linda and I don't worry about Mikey. He has all the help he needs at his place. That's because he's wealthy. It's a long story and goes all the way back to school. And I need to go back to that time now, to explain a few things.

Even before Mikey began going to school, I knew he was different. He understood things that I wasn't able to work out. He had habits that were different from anybody else. For example, my mother had a rotating set of meals. Every Tuesday he had the same meal. His meal on Wednesday was different from his meal on Tuesday, but it was the same every Wednesday. He didn't like tight clothes. Having the sun in his eyes bothered him, so my father took him out one day to try on hats that had peaks. It took four hours to find the right hat. In the end, the right hat was a yellow one that had white braiding around the bottom and an embroidered image of a parrot on the front. Mikey wore the hat all summer when he was four. But then he decided that he wanted to wear it all winter as well. Our mother had other ideas, but after a long tantrum, she agreed.

I took Mikey to school his first day. I'm not sure he wanted to go, but he didn't say anything. He wore his hat. Our parents probably talked to the teacher beforehand because Mikey had his own seat away from the other children. He wore his hat all day even in the school. The teacher tried to talk him out of it, but that didn't work. And then there was the business of touching. There were a few screaming matches until everyone learned not to touch him or even bump or brush against him, but then everything settled down. My mother arranged things so that I would always be in the same room as Mikey, at least for the first couple of years he was at school. Mikey would look at me whenever something was not quite right. That included him not understanding what the teacher wanted him to do. But he learned quickly. After just a year he could read better than some of the children who had been in school two or even three years. But he did things at his own pace and in his own way.

At school, there was only one serious incident. It involved a boy named Paul who seemed to dislike Mikey right from the start. There was nothing specific that Paul did, although I heard him more than once talking about Mikey, calling him a freak, and making fun of his hat, which Paul referred to as a dunce cap. Apart from that, nothing specific, until one day in our classroom Paul began pulling faces at Mikey. Up to that point Mikey had just ignored him. Then he started calling Mikey a freak in the open, out loud. He grabbed Mikey's cap, waved it around, and began pointing at him and laughing. But when Paul began punching Mikey on the shoulder and pushing him around, causing Mikey to wail and scream, I had to do something. I pushed Paul against the wall and told him to stop it. He tried to hit me but missed. Then I kicked him in the 'thing', and when he doubled over saying "Ow! Ow!" I started hitting him.

His nose began to bleed. He fell onto the floor, and I kicked him. I kept on kicking him. Soon there was blood everywhere, and I still remember my feelings of power and revenge. Of course, the teacher returned to the room, saw me beating Paul, stopped the fighting, and sent Mikey and me home. I don't remember the details. I do remember how good it felt to protect my little brother. I remember quite a few of the other students crying. And I remember the long and very cold talk my father had with me, and how even he was taken aback when I said that if Paul bothered Mikey again I would do the same thing only much worse. I think it was then that my father realized I hadn't acted at all in an unprovoked way. I know that he spoke to someone at the school, and a few days later when Mikey and I went back, Paul wasn't there.

It was just a couple of months after that trauma when I noticed a difference in Mikey. I worried at first. Maybe he was affected by me beating Paul, I thought. But it wasn't that. Mikey had started to become restless. He didn't want to do the reading the teacher asked. I spent more time with him, reading the pages with him that the teacher had marked. Mikey hardly ever smiled. But he didn't frown either. Eventually I became aware that whenever Mikey was having trouble doing something, he would become restless.

We had art classes. The teacher came into the room carrying a large armful of paper that was discoloured around the edges. The pieces of paper were larger than the ones our father used at home to write letters. The teacher said that a big pile of this paper had been found at the back of a storage cabinet, that it was the sort of paper nobody used any more but that it would be good for art. That paper lasted a long time. But Mikey used way more paper than anyone else. It wasn't that he wasted it, he just drew so many images. I knew very early that Mikey was a natural artist. One day, during our first year at school, we saw two cars in the street near the school crash into each other. I don't remember anyone being hurt. But there was a lot of noise. That afternoon, Mikey drew fifteen pictures showing cars in accidents. Each was only a few lines, but every one of them spoke of action. I could tell by the look on the teacher's face that she was surprised. And right away she went into the store room and came out with a large box of paper.

"Here, Mikey", she said. "This is your paper."

Then, one day, all of a sudden, and not too long after Mikey had received his box of paper, he stopped being restless. He became quiet, and even more focused than usual. A couple of days after that, he began producing some distinctive images. Very soon, his drawings became more elaborate, and even at my young age I knew that they were good, sophisticated, elegant, perhaps even professional. The teacher was impressed and left another large pile of the special paper on Mikey's desk. He would draw all day, stopping only for twenty minutes or so to do his reading, then go back to drawing. Right from the start, his drawings were detailed and interesting. Nobody knew what they meant, but everyone was attracted to them. Sometimes they looked like birds landing in odd ways. Sometimes they looked like stubby fish trying to touch their tails to their noses. Sometimes they looked like big sets of ears. And sometimes they were just interesting patterns that didn't remind me of anything in particular. He drew them in pencil for about two weeks, then he switched to crayons, and the colours and combinations of colours he used made everybody take a second, a third, and even a fourth look.

After he had been in school about a year, Mikey began learning words. And these weren't just ordinary words. He soon knew words that I hadn't seen before, even though I was two years older. We knew that he was learning words because he started using them. At first, his sentences seemed odd when they included some of these words. But then I noticed my mother and father looking at him in a strange way, the way people look at something they've never seen before and didn't expect anything like it to appear before them in just the way it did.

Then when he was eight years old, Mikey's rather laborious printing became smooth, and over a period of only six or eight months, it became writing. Not cursive handwriting. He was still printing, but his letters and words flowed. He was becoming a calligrapher. Increasingly, he used longer and more complicated words and sentences, and he was producing cohesive paragraphs which began extending to half a page or more.

By then, he was writing and drawing in almost every spare moment at home. He still wrote and drew at school, and all but a few of the things he produced he brought home. Mikey gave me a few of his drawings, and pages of his writing. I saved them all. My mother and father had some as well, or at least copies. Mikey kept all his other drawings and his writing. Each page of writing was folded once, neatly, and placed in a shoebox. He didn't fold his drawings. He stored them in an old suitcase under his bed. Each January he closed the shoebox he had used for the previous year and began filling a new shoebox. He put the previous year's shoebox in the bottom of our closet. I think my mother must have looked at them when Mikey was at school and decided that they should be kept. But she couldn't actually take any of them. Nobody was allowed to do that. Mikey didn't want anybody to look in his shoeboxes. I suppose that my mother took a few of them off secretly to the library, or somewhere, when Mikey and I were at school, and made copies.

Apart from drawing and reading and some simple arithmetic, Mikey had such difficulty learning anything that he just attended school in whatever grade came next, but wasn't required to sit exams. As long as he could draw and read and write, Mikey was perfectly happy. My father began buying Mikey books to read, as well as books that showed different sorts of drawings. Mikey looked at them all. He read all the books, and he looked at all the drawings, but it seemed that his own drawings became just more and more elaborate forms of the kinds of things he had always drawn. The difference was that his use of colours became increasingly arresting, inventive, and provocative in the creative sense.

When Mikey was ten years old, my father convinced him to have a selection of his drawings submitted to some art competitions. Our father made all the preparations, made sure the rules were observed, and prepared and sent off the artwork that Mikey selected. Mikey's submission to *Kids Art Contest* won first prize. His submission to *World Wide Kids Drawings* was awarded third prize. The work our father sent off to the *UNESCO Louis François International Art Contest* won first prize. Our father had the award announcements framed and they were hung in our bedroom. I think Mikey looked at them once, but after that he paid no attention to them.

Mikey's drawings became more and more complex, more elaborate, and some of them were exquisite. He didn't mind me looking at them after he had finished them, but then he just put them away in the big suitcase. I asked him when I was fifteen if I could have one. He thought about it for a long time, then wanted to know why. I told him that I thought he was a great artist and that quite a few of his drawings made me feel very happy. That was one of the very few times I remember Mikey smiling, and he said okay. But he wouldn't let me look through them myself. He insisted on bringing them out of their suitcase one at a time and letting me look at them without touching them. I picked one and had it framed. But Mikey didn't want it hanging in any spot where he would always see it, so we hung it in our father's den, someplace Mikey hardly ever went.

By then, Mikey had learned how to use a computer, something I thought might never happen. In fact, he became good at writing text on his computer. And he also became good at searching for things. I saw him working on the computer one day and asked him if he wanted any help.

"No thanks."

"Okay. Can I watch?"

"Yes."

What I saw was somebody who was entirely focused. He would search for a while, then look at something on his screen and make a note on the paper next to his keyboard. He had asked if he could bring home some of the paper he used in school for drawing, and the teacher said yes, and gave him a plastic bag that must have had a thousand sheets of that old paper in it.

Late in the summer the year I was seventeen, I began getting ready to go to university. I promised my mother that I would select and pack everything that I was taking with me and place all my other clothes in a large box, so that she could decide whether anything might be kept for Mikey and what to do with the rest of them. As I was doing this, I looked in the closet that Mikey and I had shared for quite a few years, to make sure that I had left nothing there.

All Mikey's shoeboxes were gone.

I looked under his bed. No suitcase.

"I burned them."

That was all he said when I asked him where his pages of writing and his drawings were.

I was aghast. All those beautiful drawings…

Not too long before I left to go to university, I mentioned the shoeboxes and the suitcase to my mother, saying 'what a waste', or something similar.

She smiled.

"Yes. He did put them out to be burned."

What she meant by that was that he placed them in the large bin outside the back door that contained odd pieces of wood and other stuff not easy to recycle. My father used what was in that bin whenever he started the big stone barbecue that he used many times every summer when we cooked and ate meals outside.

"I found them. They're safe. I put them in the attic. Don't tell Mikey."

I was very much surprised at just how relieved I felt. We both knew they were safe where they were because Mikey was afraid of the basement, and especially of the attic, and he wouldn't go there ever.

"Do you mind if I look at them sometime?"

"No. Not at all", she said.

And I did look at them. That's when I found that Mikey had produced more than just random pages of text and a large collection of drawings. In one of the shoeboxes there was the manuscript for a book. A book that Mikey had written. I spent quite a few hours looking at Mikey's manuscript. Then I asked my mother if I could take it and some of Mikey's drawings with me to the university. She said yes, but made me promise not to lose or damage anything. There was no risk of that happening.

Over the next three months I went through his drawings and I read and reread his manuscript. It had no title. There were twenty-three chapters, not given chapter titles, just numbers. I spent a lot of time thinking about his writing and his drawing. And it was in the text of Mikey's book that I found the clue to many of his drawings. The book, in fact, was extraordinary. Not only did I read it several times that year, I made quite a few notes on it, and developed a plan that I discussed with my parents.

You've probably worked out by now that Mikey is 'on the spectrum'. We would have said at one time that he is autistic, until it was recognized that 'autism' isn't just one simple condition, that a whole complex of conditions is involved, and that a one-word characterisation is too blunt, as well as being simplistic and unfair. And even referring to this as a 'condition' is not good. For most people 'on the spectrum', it's just part of who they are. All this figured into my plan, and I talked about that too with my parents when I came home for a couple of weeks after final exams. They were sceptical at first, but when I read them several of Mikey's passages, showed them an outline of the contents, and passed around a first mock-up for a cover, their scepticism vanished.

By this time, Mikey was no longer at school. He was living at home, but in a way that gave him almost complete independence. I continued to talk to him regularly. It was clear that he was happy, in the way that Mikey always had been happy.

"Have you approached Mikey at all about this?" my mother asked, referring to my project involving his manuscript and drawings.

"In an oblique way, yes. He really isn't interested."

"No? What did he say?"

"He just said to me that he had done all that. It was finished. That he was doing other things now."

"Other things?" my father asked. "We've seen several of his recent pieces of art. Did he say anything more about that?"

I knew that Mikey talked to our parents about his work only a little, and on rare occasions, giving few details. He seemed to be more open with me, and he and I had had some discussions on the odd occasion when I came home from university, but he didn't really want to be drawn out about what he was doing or why. He just described it as 'my work'.

I talked about my Mikey project some more with my parents. By that time, I was convinced that it should be a book. My parents agreed, but they were concerned about going ahead without some sort of agreement from Mikey. We talked about that and agreed that I would bring it to the point where it would be clear whether there was interest in it on the part of a publisher.

That's where I left things with them.

Every spare hour I had I put into Mikey's book. As I worked on it, I realized how much I loved Mikey, my brother, although he would never respond to love in a way that might be expected. I realized also that I was proud of him. I had spoken to people at the Autism Society, had dug out several books, and soon knew quite a bit about what made Mikey what and who he was. But above all, he was my brother.

One of the students in my class at the university told me about his father who had published four books of fiction. I told him a little about the book my brother had written and asked if I could speak to his father. Less than two weeks later, I was in the study of William Benson. I knew nothing about him apart from what his son Andrew had told me, and until I borrowed one from the library, I had not known about his books.

He laughed when I made my rather awkward apology at not having read any of his books.

"I'm not surprised", he said, smiling. "My books have sold fairly well, but I doubt that I will ever get rich from them."

Judging from their house, the number of books in his study, and the fact that his son never seemed to be short of cash, Mr. Benson had no money worries. I found that I was curious to know how he funded his writing. But I didn't ask anything. Instead, I explained about Mikey, the book he had written, his artwork, and how I had tried to put the text and some drawings together.

"I wonder if you would be good enough to take a look at it", I asked him. "I think that Mikey has some talent, and I would like to see his book published. But I have no idea whether that's realistic."

"Yes, I would be pleased to take a look at it."

I passed the manuscript to Mr. Benson. I had scanned about thirty of Mikey's drawings, incorporated them into the text, converted the whole thing to a 6x9 book format, and given the manuscript a working title: 'On Paper'. For the cover, I had chosen one of Mikey's simplest but most vibrant drawings, a drawing that was another modification on what seemed to be his standard format.

Mr. Benson raised an eyebrow slightly when he saw the cover illustration, but then began reading the first few pages. After a few minutes, he looked up at me, wearing an odd expression, almost quizzical. He returned to the book, and over the next twenty minutes he opened it at several places and read briefly.

He closed the book gently, placed it on his desk, and looked squarely at me.

"This is most interesting", he said. "Original. Has it had any editing apart from what you might have done?"

I shook my head.

"Have you shown it to any publisher?"

"No. I wanted to get a neutral impression from someone first. Do you think it could be published?"

"I think it's crying out to be published. Do you know where your brother got the material for his text?"

"The material?"

"You've obviously read the book right through. Haven't you?"

"Yes."

"Then you will know that the text here on paper sizes and watermarks is very unusual, uncommon, things that few people know about. Certainly not at the level of detail given here. Are you saying that your brother found all this material himself?"

"I suppose so. I haven't asked him."

I told Mr. Benson about Mikey and his past.

Mr. Benson picked up the book and looked through it once more. We talked a bit more about the practicalities of having something published. But eventually, it looked like we were finished.

"Well, thank you for your time, Mr. Benson", I said, then rose, preparing to leave.

"What do you want to do with this?" Mr. Benson asked, glancing at the book mockup. "We should have some sort of plan before you leave."

"Well, I need to go away and think about how to have it published", I said, thinking about some of the things Mr. Benson had said and suggested over the previous hour or so.

"May I suggest that something more specific than that is needed? And allow me to suggest, also, that I can help with that", Mr. Benson said, "and I really do want to help."

I sat down again, and we talked for another forty-five minutes.

In the end, I agreed to have Mr. Benson approach his publisher. Right on the spot, he picked up the phone, and soon was into a discussion with a Ms. Andreotti.

"Fine", he said into the telephone, after checking with me that the arrangements I had overheard were acceptable. "We'll come to your office the day after tomorrow. Ten o'clock. Thanks Marsha. Yes. See you then."

After he had put down the phone, we talked for another fifteen minutes. Benson was convinced that Mikey's book would be a winner. He asked me to tell him more about how it had all come about. I described Mikey's first months in school, how it became evident quite soon that he was a natural artist, that the teacher had given him his own large supply of paper, and that then he just drew pictures, and starting a few years later began to write.

I had worked out part of the story.

"In the box of paper Mikey was given, there was an envelope. There was a small piece of paper in it, about the size of a decal. In fact", I said, pulling it from my shirt pocket, "it was this piece of paper." And I handed it over to Mr. Benson.

"I'm fairly sure this is where Mikey got the original idea for the basic image he used."

"It is indeed", Benson said. "Well, at least, it seems evident to me that that's the case. You know from reading your brother's text that this image is one example of a cap worn by a Fool. Do you know what a watermark is?"

"I have some idea", I said, but when I thought more about it I realized that it was only a word I had heard, and I took it in as a piece of implicit information without asking any further.

Benson explained it to me at some length.

"But this image", he said, "what you've just handed me. On its own, it probably would mean nothing to most people. But from what I've been able to see in just a brief look at your brother's text, he knows a great deal about this image, its background. He knows, for instance, that it's the Fool's Cap. And he knows that it was used as the watermark on a certain size of paper. That watermark hasn't been used for that specific paper size for a long time. In fact, it was discontinued for that in 1795, to be exact."

"Why did they use that picture?"

"I don't know", Mr. Benson said. He sat there for a moment looking at his bookshelves, thinking.

"How did that picture come to be in the box of paper that was given to Mikey?" I asked.

"I would love to know that", Mr. Benson said. "I expect that somebody put it there, somebody who knew some history, maybe somebody who had a project in mind but never got round to it."

I was puzzled, and it must have been obvious. Mr. Benson focused on me, appearing to collect his thoughts.

"That watermark, the Fool's Cap, was used on only one size of paper, and that size of paper came to be known as foolscap. It was in common use in Britain and in Canada. I can just remember using paper in school that our teacher called foolscap. It never occurred to me to ask why it had that name. But then if I had asked, probably the teacher wouldn't have known. So it's really quite impressive that your brother not only wondered about that picture, but that he did enough digging to realize that it was a Fool's Cap. But then he must have learned, somehow, that it was used on a particular type of paper. Then, once again, he must have found out somehow that that paper itself was called foolscap. And finally, he must have decided, somehow, based on what you've said, that the paper he'd been given for his drawing was in fact piles of old foolscap that had been hidden for decades in some cupboard."

Mr. Benson stopped, looked again at Mikey's manuscript, smiled, and shook his head.

"Just a quick look at this book", and he glanced again at the mockup he had just been thumbing through, "indicates to me that your brother not only has a unique sort of mind but that he's also quite intelligent. I'm sure that, in his shoes, *I* wouldn't have asked the right questions and been able to find what he has found."

Mr. Benson made a note about our meeting with his publisher and handed it to me. Then I left. My meeting with Mr. Benson had made me determined now that Mikey's work would be published.

We had our meeting with Mr. Benson's publisher. Ms. Andreotti was all business, but she said that based on just a fifteen-minute scan of the manuscript, plus her discussion with me and Mr. Benson, she was taking the unusual step of accepting the manuscript for review. No literary agent needed.

"Who will be doing the review?" Mr. Benson asked.

"I will", she replied without hesitation.

Ms. Andreotti's review took little time. There were three more meetings. Two weeks later I received a letter, copied to Mr. Benson, saying that the publisher wanted to sign a contract for Mikey's book.

My parents and I spoke to Mikey about his book. He agreed to everything we were doing, but it was clear that he was agreeing simply from lack of interest. For him, this was all in the past. It was something he had finished and was done with. An agreement was drawn up giving me the authority to make all decisions concerning Mikey's book. I explained it to him. But even before I had finished the explanation, he waved at me impatiently.

"Okay. Let me sign it."

Things happened quickly after that. I spoke to various organizations involved in autism. I left each of them a copy of the publisher's letter to me and a three page summary of Mikey's book and how it had come into being. Their responses were overwhelming.

Just a few months later, Mikey's book was published. It seemed that I was asked to talk about it to everyone. Sales of the book rocketed skywards, but none of that had anything to do with me. It was Mikey's book, the story of how it had come into existence, and the general level of interest in people like Mikey. Three quarters of the revenue we received from book sales went into a fund for Mikey. That's how he became wealthy. The remaining quarter was shared among three organizations involved in autism.

I still have Mikey's cap. His Fool's Cap. He hasn't worn it for decades. I pull it out every now and then and look at it. It reminds me so much of all the things that Mikey and I shared. From my own perspective, it makes me think again, every time, about what Mikey did, how he got to the bottom of something that, without him, wouldn't have been even a mystery, would simply have been passed by unnoticed. From that single image, and from the word 'foolscap', Mikey extracted a rich piece of social history. And he showed me that in many of our words, in the everyday things around us, there are treasures of meaning.

I continue to make sure that Mikey is okay.

He's my brother.

Petard

It was a Tuesday, mid-April, at 1:30 am when I heard the two dull thuds. I had just climbed into bed after filing a story. So, I climbed out of bed again, because I knew that this was more than just somebody dropping a couple of pounds of butter on the next floor up.

Our condo building is nine storeys. An older structure. Great design. Well run. So, a very nice place to live, and a fabulous investment. My ex-wife, Donna, lives just a few blocks away. We get along very well, but recognized soon after our wedding that our lives simply didn't mesh, and never would do so, and a quiet amicable separation and divorce was the only thing that made sense. Donna doesn't have any one man in her life, in any serious way. She has quite a few of them in a way that's a bit less serious. And that's where things are a little strange.

Because I'm one of those men.

I know. I know. It sounds odd. But it works. And I learned long ago to be slow about questioning something that works. Well, actually, it does more than just work.

We really get along, both in and out of bed.

That night, Donna wasn't with me.

I was still buttoning my shirt when I reached the elevator lobby. A quick glance at the indicators revealed that both elevators were at the parking garage level. So, down the stairs to the ground floor. The concierge wasn't there. I pushed through the lobby doors and headed around toward the public entrance to the parking garage, not wanting to be told by anybody that I couldn't do this or that, couldn't go here or there. I'm a journalist, for God's sake. But also a private investigator, for God's sake. I need to know.

A figure was hurrying past just as I left the lobby. Tall. Grey hair. Blue suit. Looking around furtively. I backed up against the wall and waited for him to disappear into the passageway leading to King Street.

I didn't want him to see me. More particularly, I didn't want him to know that I had seen him. Because I knew him on sight, and seeing him scurrying off the way he was doing just confirmed for me that his presence flagged something significant.

I sprinted to the public entrance to the parking garage, loped down the stairs, and could smell it even before I reached the glass door leading into the garage proper. A strong burnt smell.

The concierge was walking quickly, urgently, along the central lane of the parking garage, trying vainly to raise someone on his cellphone. But being thirty feet underground made that impossible. Once he had moved along such that my location was out of his peripheral vision, I opened the door and moved into the garage. The burnt smell was very strong, and there was smoke hugging the ceiling. It seemed that the smoke was coming from the right, so I threaded among the parked cars, moving in that direction. Just then the fire alarm activated, most likely because smoke had reached the nearest detector. Rounding one of the structures that contained a stairwell, I could see the concierge further along, heading for the stairwell nearest to him and toward the source of the smoke. Probably intending to get a slightly better look, then go up a floor, or maybe go outside, to get a signal. When he had vanished into the stairwell, I sprinted along the car park, and then saw it.

What had once been a Lexus was now a pile of junk. Its roof had been blown off, and the entire front end of the car was a total wreck, the wheels ripped off, the radiator pushed out of the grill, coolant running down toward the drain.

All around the car there was powder on the garage floor. I ran up to the wreckage, had a quick look at it from several angles, wetted a finger, touched it to one of the areas on the floor where the powder was thickest, raised the finger to my face, sniffed, and touched the tip of my tongue.

At that point, I turned and ran back to the public entrance to the garage, raced up the steps, ran north into King Street, and turned left. But I did all this only after taking a quick series of photos.

Over a cup of coffee at Basil's Brew, I thought over what I had just seen.

"Up late?" Basil asked, making barista conversation, not necessarily expecting an answer.

"Worked late. Then couldn't sleep. Came along for your coffee and dulcet tones."

Basil snorted, and carried on with the endless task of wiping down surfaces.

An image returned to me of the tall, grey-haired man who had appeared to be coming out of the parking garage. I had seen him before, quite a few times. And every time I saw him he had that look of not wanting anybody to take notice of him. In my business, or rather, in my businesses, one keeps an eye out for things or people who reappear. And it seemed that he had always been coming out of the parking garage. Fair enough. People park there all the time, often to repeat the same tasks, attend the same business meetings, complete the same routines.

But the voice in my ear said that there was something more involved. And the voice is my friend. My trustworthy friend.

One other thing.

The powder on the parking garage floor was heroin.

It's rarely possible to do work for a client and to report one's findings from that work in the press. Clients tend to have this overwhelming shyness of the Fourth Estate. Not that they have fears of being caught out in something shady! Good grief, no! These are upstanding corporations we're talking about! No, I think it's just a desire to be as close to invisible as possible, thereby avoiding the Fickle Finger of Fate, the machinations of competitors, and all the enemies that maraud in that jungle they call 'the World of Business'. Who are those enemies? People, organizations, who believe that the world is a great zero-sum game, that if my competitor stumbles, I can run faster. What form do those enemies assume? Take your pick, but my guesses are giant snakes, giant spiders, and big cats.

But it's always possible to do a job for a client and keep a weather eye open for lucrative journalistic angles. It can work the other way, too. Opportunities abound. But one has to be able to spot them. The more of these opportunities one finds, the greater the chance of being able to earn a crust, or to turn a groat, as a landlady long ago was fond of saying.

And so it was that after the fourth time I had seen Tall Blue Suit hastening from our building's parking garage, I found the opportunity to make good use of my camera. It's amazing what one can learn once one has a photo. TBS turned out to be known as James Herman, almost certainly not his real name, but enough for a start. Sitting in Basil's little caffeine oasis, enjoying the wee hours and having the place almost to myself, I checked the most recent results of my photographic prowess, something I hoped would land me yet another information fish.

"Stan", I said pleasantly into my cellphone. "How are things?"

Things were fine, or as fine as they could be for an insomniac policeman at something after 2 am on an unremarkable Tuesday.

Stan and I had a longstanding agreement that involved mutual back-scratching and pocket-lining. It worked well. Itches were relieved and lucre was exchanged. This time, I had asked Stan to get me the gen on a car licence number, and indeed, the very car that was now a wreck in our parking garage.

"Where are you now?" Stan asked. "At Basil's?"

"Yes."

"Okay. I'll see you there in fifteen minutes."

Stan is easy to miss in a crowd, unless one knows him well. He always wears a slightly baggy grey coat, and he has a pasty face, no distinguishing features, and the kind of salt-and-pepper hair commonly found on men ranging from their early thirties to their late sixties. Mr. Invisibility. But Stan is a gem. He has a sharp mind and he likes putting away the bad guys, but he is also well aware that the world is a catch-as-catch-can place, and that successful cowboys in white hats exist only in the movies. So Stan, like me, is one for just wading into the fray, eyes open and elbows out, and we are both convinced that this is the way to make the world a better place and at the same time to put beer in the fridge. Really nothing more than Adam Smith at work.

Stan slid onto the seat beside me like a ghost. He smiled at Basil, who placed in front of Stan the coffee I had asked him to have ready.

"Anything exciting?" Stan asked, subdued as usual, like someone inquiring about the price of fennel bulbs.

Without saying anything, I showed Stan the three pictures I had taken of the wrecked Lexus, giving him a one-sentence summary of when and where.

"And the white powder?"

"None other", I replied.

Stan just nodded.

"The car is owned by a numbered Ontario company. The principal in the company is someone named Jerome Smith."

"Well", I said, "at least the Jerome part is original."

"Did you know the car from somewhere?" Stan asked.

"No. They always use a different car, but they've got a bit sloppy lately. It's always TBS who appears later, but the past three interactions seem to have involved the same delivery man."

"So, what happened this time?" Stan asked. "A deal gone wrong?" Stan asked.

"Or maybe a deal sabotaged. Perhaps somebody deliberately made things look too obvious. I don't know."

Stan nodded again.

"You going to give them a prod?" he asked.

It was my turn to nod, as I found the paragraphs I had produced on my phone and showed them to Stan. He read silently for a couple of minutes.

"I think you've got it all", Stan said. "Are you going to post it?"

"Yes. Right now." And as I said this I sent off the story and one picture to one of the hot-shot online news rags I write for. My byline would bring in responses almost immediately, proof that these rags were watched closely by the police and by their underworld sparring partners.

"Were you able to get a track on Herman?"

"In the bag", Stan replied.

"Do we know where he fences stuff?"

"Yes. Several places. But product like this probably goes to just one buyer."

"We have all the information we need? We know who and where?"

"Oh yes!" Stan said with some evident satisfaction.

"And the intervenor? The competition, it will be assumed, who has stymied this particular exchange? We know everything we need to know, I'm assuming, where and how much?"

Another nod from Stan.

"Okay. I guess now we just wait."

Stan and I chatted for another few minutes, then Stan looked at his watch and said he had to get back. We didn't talk about money, but we knew the payment would come in very soon. We also knew that our involvement in this line of work would end here for a decent interval.

It had been stupid of Herman to keep doing the same routine so many times. If I hadn't seen the pattern, someone else would have done so quite soon. But I had seen it. In fact, I even had worked out their schedule, for delivering a car to the parking garage, and then someone else arriving later to drive it out. This was never done at predictable intervals, but there was a pattern, and I had found it. The swap was always done at night, and the car never was driven out of the parking garage before two o'clock in the morning. But Herman was now toast. His fence was out on probably a kilogram of heroin, and Herman had only one course open to him. He had to become scarce very quickly, But the chances were that he wouldn't be able to do this quickly enough.

Herman's fate would be wrapped up very soon, but the full word on what had happened wouldn't be out on the street for a few days. Long enough for the intervenor to render financial thanks to an accomplice, unknown to the intervenor, for putting a big spike into a competitor's distribution network. It was a risky game, but it paid off at a societal level by having one more of those purveyors of misery out of play.

Sweetest of all, Stan and I both saw this result at close range, first hand, and at very little personal risk. We also pocketed our share.

And it had cost me very little to hire someone, at a long arm's-length, to rig the two pieces of C-4 in that car.

When the phone rang sometime later, I was pretty sure it would be Donna. It was, and I slipped into another life.

Theatre

David smiled at me as we watched people filing in, taking an inordinate amount of time to decide which of the three hundred seats, all equally good, they would occupy.

Here we were again, in the Pentangle Theatre, surrounded by logos — colourful, stylized five-pointed star figures, all of different sizes, many of them asymmetrical. And, as always, the stream of theatregoers gradually filled the seats in the performing space, while music reminiscent of the eponymous 1960s band filled the air.

David and I did this regularly, about every two weeks, not always at the Pentangle, of course. We attended a performance of something, usually somewhat fringe in nature, but almost always promising an element that would catch our imaginations.

That evening we would see the first of four performances of a one-act play called *Catalytic Sex*. The programme notes gave nothing away, which seemed to irritate a few of the other patrons, but struck what we thought was exactly the right note.

"Just what they needed to do", David said.

"No spoon-feeding, right?"

"Way too much of that going around. It's some sort of complex", David pronounced, nodding to confirm that his response had been definitive, a statement to end discussion.

"Well…", I began.

"Ah!" David piped up in conversational revival, smiling brightly. "What incipient disputation breaks from yonder whatever?"

The last of the patrons had entered. The doors were closed. The music faded, but we didn't.

"Not complex", I said. "More like simplex."

"Okay", David responded, ready to take argumentative flight. "You're thinking of herpes, no doubt."

"Hermes? Yes, of course. Thrice-greatest", I blundered on, hoping he would rise to this deviation, thrash around a bit, perhaps stub a few cerebral toes.

"No. Not Hermes. Herpes, you dolt!"

"Yes, of course", I said, the dolt retrieving the scent. "Those poor souls afflicted by mental cold sores."

"Now you're getting closer. But simplex, as in the much misused word 'linear', as in eschewing complexity, as in stamping out uncertainty, as in fearing loose-ended incompleteness, as in denying any of that stuff called subtlety, as in —"

"Why do you always take the long way round?" I whined, embarking once more on a favoured theme. "Why not just say, er, something like, um — "

Just then the lights began to go down.

"Sounds perfect!" David declared. "Why didn't I think of that?"

"Shhh!"

"Is that a rattlesnake I hear?" David said in a loud whisper, trepidation adding a juvenile tremolo to his voice.

"I hope not. It's right behind us."

"Shhhh!!"

"You've upset it now", David said. "How different our world would look today had you been present in Eden."

"Shhhhh!!! Quiet, you two!"

"Thank heaven!" David said. "It can't be a rattlesnake."

"No. But it still could be a snake. Maybe it has some apples."

We waited ten seconds. Then the lights came up, the actors were in place. David and I sighed happily. Too late for the snake to respond now. How satisfying it is to get in the last word!

The action on stage went horizontal quickly enough. The dialogue was good, when dialogue was needed. The premise was interesting, turning on the meaning of the Greek root common to the words 'catalysis' and 'analysis'. This harked back, we were both convinced, to the notion of setting something free, while at the same time being chained heavy-handedly to things Freudian. That idea then informed the play's structure and action so as to reveal the thoughts, wishes, and expectations of the characters.

We filed out of the theatre ahead of all the others, who remained squirming in their seats, muttering querulously, apparently in the grip of a quest for programs, or for lose change, car keys, things that rattle.

"I liked the references", I said. "Song of Solomon, Catullus, Juvenal, John Cleland, D. H. Lawrence, Swinburne, and right through to Beardsley and others. Brilliant. Everything from the garden of the classically erotic to good old *nostalgie de la boue*."

"I liked the long scene of the two in bed", David recalled, smiling, "him obliviously reciting stuff in Greek at great length, and the other him in a state of pre-copulatory anxiety."

"And the regular ejaculations 'Sapristi!' and 'Caleçon!'"

"I thought they were more like exclamations", David corrected.

"No", I countered. "Too weak. Interjections, at the very least."

As we headed for the exit, we felt pursued, as usual, by a throng of people trying to figure out what they had just seen and wondering, as they listened to us, whether they had fallen asleep and missed all the juicy bits. Leaving the theatre building, we walked toward the nearest tram stop, then decided just to continue on foot.

"What would you say?" I asked. "B+?"

"That's about right. The middle third could have been more lively."

"But it was well done", I added. "Good, competent theatre."

We walked further, and I was sure that David was doing the same as me, rerunning scenes from the play in his head.

"Back to the old usual tomorrow, hey?"

"Yes", I said, with muted enthusiasm. "Are you still working on the heat exchanger project?"

"I am. I'll be at the meeting tomorrow. Will you?"

"Yes. Do you think we'll need to liven it up?" I asked.

"No. Further back than that. I think we'll need to resuscitate it."

We went our separate ways.

The meeting room we entered next morning was too big. It accommodated the six people who needed to be present, but also provided seating space for the nine who had brought no notepad or pen, those whose presence was nominally legitimate but who had known for a long time that attending meetings saved having to work, those who would warm seats on behalf of absent 'stakeholders', or those who had no need whatever to be there, as far as we could see.

The chairman brought the meeting to order and immediately began counting rivets — David's term for discussing fine details when the reason for doing so remains unknown.

"Is there an agenda?" I asked.

"Oh!" the chairman sputtered, hands full of metaphorical rivets but having lost count. He stood before the whiteboard, magic marker poised, and no women being present, he then scratched his crotch contentedly and said he had forgotten to bring it.

"My dull brain was wrought with things forgotten", David muttered, quoting from *Macbeth*.

"Sorry David. I didn't catch that", the chairman said, waving a hand in apology.

"My apologies, Mr. Chairman. I said 'full strain is what the O-rings are for.'"

"Ah! Yes! The O-rings. Thank you for reminding me." And the discussion then began to lumber over that hill.

David slid his notepad toward me. He had written three words:

"*mortals' chiefest enemy*", more Macbeth

I smiled and nodded, added a line, then passed it back to him:

"*The sense of danger must not disappear*", which continued with the same theme but leaped three centuries ahead to Auden

David quickly penned beneath it:

"*The dirt, the imprecision, and the beer*", more Auden, oddly suited to engineering

My reply read:

"*Perfection of a kind was what he was after*", yet more Auden but badly aimed

Eager to make another leap, David scribbled:

"*So here he was without maps or supplies,*
A hundred miles from any decent town"

Vintage Auden. The meeting in a nutshell.

"You make a good point, Jim", the chairman said to one of those around the table and to the room at large. "Anyone have a comment on that? No? What about you, David? You seem to be able to come up with the right thing at the right time."

"Well, Mr. Chairman", David began, having heard none of the exchange in question, "my sense is that hopes of quietly inheriting the Earth are likely misplaced. We can't hold back. We must rise like lions after slumber. Here's what I think."

And he then went into a long outline for a design change.

"Hmmm. Interesting. Very interesting. Well worth taking a look at."

The chairman, apparently hoping to be tossed a life ring, then turned to another individual.

"Archie. Your group is the design authority. Could you take that suggestion away and do an assessment?"

Archie looked up from what appeared to be a page of doodles, scratched his head, trying to remember what day it was, then nodded vaguely, as though saying 'yes' to relish but please hold the onions.

Eventually, the meeting broke up. David and I had passed our notepad back and forth many times more. We had outlined a number of next steps, none discussed at the meeting, but we would pass them on to the chairman, a nice enough guy who deserved at least that much support.

We walked toward our offices.

"What's your take?" I asked.

"Not more than a C", David replied. "Getting close to opening night, but that sounded more like an early run-through. Amateur theatre. Not more than that."

Back in our side of the building, George, our manager, waved from his office.

"David! Michael! Could I see you for a minute?"

We went in, and in response to his hand signal I closed the door.

"I'll be talking to the designers later, but I wanted your input. You've made a number of good suggestions on the heat exchanger project, and I wanted your informal feedback. You are, after all, not officially involved in the project, just occasional outside reviewers", and here he smiled knowingly, "so you can be more independent, more unbiased, have a more unique view than most."

He smiled again, an all-us-guys-together smile, gliding in ignorance away from his disastrous word misuse just as Alexander had marched past a group of low hills, unaware that they were the buried ruins of Nineveh.

George's questions indicated that his understanding was of the 'glass darkly' type. But we gave him straight answers, hoping we had interpreted his hazy questions correctly.

He made a few notes, drew an authoritative line across his pad, dropped his pencil, then leaned back in his chair.

"I know I've asked you both before, but I'll ask again. Shouldn't you be considering applying for managerial positions? My people all agree that you have what it takes."

We both repeated the cases we had made against this development many times already, something that George and others had either not heard, not understood, or forgotten.

George nodded slowly, his expression fixed, displaying all the sagacity of a Polonius.

"Well, thanks for your time, guys. And thanks for what you're contributing to this project."

He then gave a nudge-nudge wink-wink smile.

"Think about those managerial positions."

We left and began walking down the corridor.

"Your cubicle or mine?" David asked.

"Yours", I said. "It doesn't smell of old socks."

I sat in David's guest chair.

"What's your rating?" I asked.

"He's a natural, George is. At least an 'A'. Lines delivered flawlessly. Perfect timing. I don't think I've seen better theatre of the absurd."

Jump

There was something about her. I couldn't see just what. It was something that flickered, and then was gone. She looked at me again across the restaurant, a place in central Toronto not far from where I live, and then quickly looked away. Very roughly my age, somewhere in her thirties, I guessed. Medium-long chestnut hair. A prominent jaw and a slightly pointy chin.

Was it the eyes? Was it the high forehead and the distinctive, slightly masculine planes at her temples? Was it the somewhat pouty lips? But then, even as I had that thought and it flashed away, she compressed her lips as if in impatience, pulled a newspaper out of the cloth bag at her feet, opened it on the table, bent her head, and began to read. Her hair fell across the sides of her face, and from my vantage point this masked her features almost completely.

But an image had flickered tantalizingly at the back of my mind.

I immediately dug after it, chased it through some echoing corridors of memory, and then managed to grab it, turn it toward me, and look at it directly.

The image spoke to me of the past.

Summer.

By some means, I knew that I was eleven.

The image unfolded a little more.

The feeling came to me of the sun beating down on my skin.

Another flicker, and an image of my right arm appeared briefly.

My skin was swarthy thanks to the fact that I browned easily and burned only if I was quite careless.

More of the picture flashed up.

I was standing on the pedestrian walkway on the bridge that spanned the river in our village, the rough surface of its guardrail warm and familiar. I had been looking down at the river, which was always a central element of summer in my life to that point.

The water beneath me was about twelve feet deep.

I knew this because my friends and I had explored the bottom extensively.

The water flowed quickly.

I followed the direction of flow with my gaze, and there it was, a ramp, about a third of the way out from the right bank as I looked downstream.

A longer flashback appeared, this one in detail and remaining long enough for me to fix it in memory. A girl climbed up onto the railing, swung her legs over, and sat there. She was pretty and lively. I knew that she was going to jump into the river at some point, swim to the left bank, climb onto the dock, and then come back onto the pedestrian walkway and do it again. She was about three feet from me, and she knew who I was, but she paid no attention to me. She was not quite five years older than me, I guessed, and although she wasn't all that much older than me in years, physically she already had the shape and allure of girls a couple of years older than she was. She was almost a grown-up, I recalled thinking, while I was barely a few years out of diapers. To her, I was invisible.

This didn't cause me any pain or grief. I took it as just a fact of life.

She ran her hands through her shortish hair, and a light spray of water fell onto the walkway behind her. She turned to say something to a friend who was about to climb up beside her, laughed, and then adjusted the straps to her swimming top. There was a glimpse of the generous amounts of flesh that filled her top, and I was surprised to see how much it moved as she ran her thumbs under the shoulder straps. For some reason, I had thought they would be quite hard.

She and her friend had a clipped conversation, then they both launched themselves, two girls together, into the river, feet first. Once they had surfaced and began swimming toward the bank, I climbed onto the railing, jumped into the water, and began swimming toward the large ramped object that had appeared in the river just two days earlier.

It was the water ski jump, and its sloped and waxed surface was a great place to lie in the sun and allow our fingertips to recover from their prune skin condition, something that always happened after we spent more than an hour in the water.

We always knew that summer would soon close down when the water ski jump was lifted from its storage slot, lowered into the river, and towed into place and anchored. The annual watersports show would begin in a few weeks. Then the days would start becoming noticeably shorter. The water in the river would become cooler. And our euphoric sense of unending summer would be dashed by the realization that school would begin again.

Like everyone else, I wasn't immune to this. My mood would change as well.

But there was no benefit in anticipating either summer's lamentable downturn or the systematic encroachment of autumn. Best just to live for the moment. And that's what I was determined to do as the end of the summer approached.

Having swum to the ski jump, I pulled myself out of the water and lay down, head uphill, the side of my face cradled on my forearms, and let the sun do its work. I would lie there for maybe twenty minutes, then roll off into the river, swim once around the jump to cool off, climb back onto the jump, and the whole process would repeat. By five o'clock, the sun would be headed westward, I would be in a state of lassitude, and I would roll into the river one last time. After swimming to the shore, I would collect my towel from where I had left it on the dock, and drift home. There would be pro forma questions about my day from my mother, changing out of swimming trunks, wondering yet again why water seemed to make everything shrink, pulling on clean underwear, shorts, and a shirt, and getting ready for dinner. By seven o'clock there would be a lot of yawning, and I would offer no resistance to the suggestion that I go to bed.

Days would pass like that in the summer. I'm tempted to add the qualifier 'year after year', but when I look back on it there were a lot of changes, significant changes over just a couple of years, between the ages of eleven and thirteen, the last year I was allowed to while away the summer in that fashion.

Another clear memory surfaced from that year, when I was thirteen.

It was summer again, and I was sunning myself on the water ski jump. That particular day, I lay there until well after six o'clock. The air was warm, there was no wind, and the recent conversation I had had with my father made it clear that there would be pressure on me next year. One of his good friends, someone I had referred to as 'Uncle Frank', wanted a young lad to help in his woodworking shop the next year. It was time, my father suggested in a way that I couldn't deny, for me to begin exchanging a summer suntan for some summer blisters.

But that was next year.

The big question at the moment, lying on the ski jump, was whether I would go home or have one more round of swimming and sunning.

The swimming and sunning alternative won, hands down. I rolled into the water, did my circuit of the jump, climbed out again, lay down, and enjoyed the moment.

The hair on my arms, which had become satisfactorily thick over the previous year, was now bleached white. The hair on my head likewise had softened from brown to light auburn. I had begun to put on muscle mass, and I had noticed my mother looking at me several times in a speculative way. Most satisfying, though, was my deeply browned skin, something that would have raised great concern a few decades later, but I liked to think that I was the envy of the six or seven redheads my age in the village.

I felt the water ski jump rock slightly. Looking up, I saw the figure of a girl stretching out on the ski jump. (Girl or woman? I was at the age where I still wasn't sure of the difference, and couldn't decide which word to use.) Her head was turned away from me, but I knew it was Barbara, the girl from a few years earlier whose bathing suit straps I still remembered clearly. She was sufficiently older than me to be scary, and now seemed far more mature and unreachable than she had back then. I put my head down again, thinking that in ten minutes I would call it a day.

Just a few minutes later, the ski jump rocked slightly. I looked up and noticed that Barbara was no longer there. Evidently she had rolled off into the water, and I could hear her splashing her way to shore. I dozed for five minutes, then rolled into the river in turn, swam to the shore and headed home.

Overnight, something in the village changed.

I surfaced from my slumbers, heard the sound of light rain on my window, and promptly went back to sleep. At eight thirty, it was made clear to me that no more lounging would be tolerated. I rose, dressed, had breakfast, and then announced that I was going to the village library. The rain had stopped, but it was overcast, and the river had no real allure.

An hour later, my perusal of *Twenty Thousand Leagues Under the Sea* was interrupted.

By my father.

He wasn't angry. But he looked concerned.

"We're going home", he said. "Now."

When we reached home, I was surprised to see a police car parked on the street next to our house. I looked at my father. He looked back at me, smiled faintly, nodded, and indicated that we should go inside. My mother and a man in a grey suit were sitting at the table. I stopped in the doorway. I wasn't getting a good feeling about this.

"Michael", my father said. "This is Detective Anderson. He's going to ask you a few questions."

The detective smiled at me. It was a cold smile. "Please sit down, Michael", he said. I sat next to my mother on the opposite side of the table from the detective.

"You were swimming yesterday, Michael, is that correct?"

"Yes."

"Where?"

"In the river."

"And where were you swimming? Next to the dock?"

"No. I jumped off the bridge a few times, then I swam to the water ski jump and I lay there in the sun."

"How long were you lying there?"

"Well, I rolled off the jump every half hour or so to cool down, then I climbed back up on the ramp and lay in the sun again."

"And were you alone?"

"No. Murray Howard and I were together."

"For how long?"

I looked at my mother and father. They nodded for me to answer. My mother looked very stressed.

"Well, we met there at about ten thirty in the morning, and we were swimming for about two hours, then we went and had a hot dog each at the River Grill, then we went back swimming."

"And you were swimming the rest of the afternoon?"

"We swam until about four thirty, then Murray said he had to go home."

"And did you go home too?"

"Not. I stayed to do some more swimming."

"And where did you swim?"

"Well, I didn't really do much swimming. I was mostly lying on the water ski jump."

"And how long did you do that?"

"Until about five thirty. I got home at about six."

"And were you alone all that time, I mean from four thirty to five thirty?"

"Yes."

"There was nobody else there for that hour?"

"No. Well, Barbara was there for a while."

"Is that Barbara Small?"

"Yes."

"You say she was there for a while. How long? The whole hour? Half that time? Just a few minutes?"

"I … I don't know. I think it was more than a few minutes, but less than half an hour."

"And was she swimming?"

"I don't know. She climbed up onto the water ski jump and lay down."

"Did you speak to her?"

"No. She's a big kid."

"Who left first? Was it you or her?"

"I felt the ski jump move, and when I looked up she wasn't there. I guess she just rolled off into the river."

"Did you see her after that?"

I just looked at him. I was becoming really scared.

"Did you see her swim away?"

"N... No."

I knew that my lip was quivering. My father put his hand on my shoulder and squeezed.

"So she was on the water ski jump, maybe ten minutes? maybe twenty minutes? but you didn't say anything to her, and she didn't say anything to you. Is that right?"

"Yes." I looked at my hands. Then I looked up at the detective. "Why are you asking me all this?"

He just smiled.

"Thank you Michael. You've been helpful." He looked at my dad. "May I speak to you Mr. Wardell?"

My father nodded. Then they both rose and went back outside.

I looked at my mother. Tears began rolling down my cheeks. I didn't want to cry, and I was angry that it was happening. But by then I really was scared.

My mother took me in her arms and rocked me slowly, although she wasn't in much better shape than me.

About ten minutes later, my father came back inside and I could hear a car pulling away. My father sat down at the table. I wiped my cheeks dry and looked at him.

"Michael", he said. "I don't really know how to say this, but Barbara Small didn't go home last night. Nobody knows where she is. You might have been the last person to see her."

After that, something odd happened. I never heard another word about it. Not directly, that is. I was aware that people had searched the full length of the river looking for a body, but found nothing. I was aware of people talking in whispers on street corners. The whole matter was something I made great efforts to shut out of my mind.

Weeks went by before I could think about the water ski jump again. I didn't go swimming all the rest of that summer. I refused to go to the watersports show. In fact, I wouldn't go into the village for weeks because I just didn't want to see the water ski jump again.

I guess I finally got over it. I finished high school, and then it was time to leave my village and study physics at university. I got my degree and found a good job. My adult life was well underway. I kept up with a few of my boyhood friends and the only memories I had from that time were good ones.

She was still reading the paper, and her hair was still hanging down both sides of her face. I rose from my seat and went over to her table. By that time I was quite sure I knew who she was and I was curious and intrigued.

"Barbara?" I said.

There was a moment of hesitation, then she looked up.

"No. I'm afraid you have the wrong person. My name isn't Barbara."

"My apologies", I said, went back to my table, left some money for my bill, and walked out of the restaurant.

I had made it about a hundred metres down the street when I heard quick footsteps behind me. I turned to look.

She walked up to me, the woman from the restaurant.

"Michael", she said. "Can we talk?" And without waiting for an answer she put her arm through mine and moved away at a fast walk. I was pretty much obliged to go along. And I did.

We turned several corners, then went through a passageway into a pleasant internal courtyard, and she nodded toward a small pub called Benjamin's, a spot well-known to residents of central Toronto, and it occurred to me only later that she must have been a city resident to know about it. We entered, and she walked straight through and out the back, onto a patio that had space for about twenty people. We were the only ones there. We sat in the furthest corner, and when a waiter appeared I asked for a half-litre of white wine. The wine was soon delivered, and we were alone.

"You're right. I was called Barbara at one time, but now I'm Andrea Barkwell."

I took a sip of wine, but it must have been evident that I had no idea what was going on.

"You're the last person I ever wanted to see again. Not because I didn't like you. Not that at all."

She took a largish sip of wine herself.

"You remember that day on the water ski jump."

I nodded, understanding less and less as she spoke.

"I rolled off into the water", she said, "splashed around a bit, then hid underneath, in the air space between the barrels. I could feel the ski jump rocking in the water when you rolled off and swam away. I stayed there until well after dark. I nearly froze to death. Then I came out, did a breaststroke as quietly as I could to the shore, grabbed a case of things I had left hidden in some bushes, and ran away."

"Why?" I asked.

She ignored my question.

"I heard that they looked for me for quite a while. But by then I had made my way to Regina, and some people helped me get a new identity. A few years after I ran away, I learned that I had been declared legally dead."

"Why?" I asked again.

"You're the first person who has ever recognized me, Michael. I'm now going to beg you to forget all about me. Will you promise?"

I followed suit and ignored her question in turn.

"Why did you come after me just now? Why didn't you just leave that restaurant and forget about the whole thing?"

"Because", she said, "I wanted to make sure you wouldn't give me away, not even inadvertently. Please!"

"But why did you do all that, run away, change your name?"

She looked at me closely for a moment, took another sip of wine, then looked at me again.

"I had to get away from my father."

It took me only a few seconds to figure out what that meant.

"I — I'm sorry Bar — I mean Andrea."

She waved that away.

We sipped some more wine.

"Are you living here in Toronto now?" I asked.

"No. I'm here on a business trip. I really didn't want to come, but the business, you know, not really any other option. I was hoping to be in and out, here just two days. Just rotten luck that our paths should cross."

That didn't sound quite right to me. She appeared entirely comfortable in what should have been, given her statements, a large and distant city. It began to dawn on me that the woman I was with might well have lived, be living, a phantom life, most of it concocted.

"Will you promise — "

"Look, Andrea. I have no interest in giving you away."

I thought back to what had happened to her family in the years after her disappearance. She seemed to know what I was thinking.

"I hated them both. My father for what he was and what he did and tried to do, and my mother for not standing up to him. They both deserved what they got, as far as I'm concerned."

And I recalled what had happened, related to me by my parents. George Small had been savagely beaten to death. None of his face was recognizable. Two years later, Virginia Small, who had moved away to a medium-sized local city and drifted into squalor, had died from an overdose of sleeping pills.

Andrea was looking at my face. I'm sure she could tell that I knew what had happened, but her expression was completely impassive.

We finished the wine. Andrea said she had to go. I didn't ask her anything more about herself, and she didn't offer anything. She still had that something I had seen in her eyes all those years ago, and I remembered that barely pubescent boy, gaining his first glimpse at a pair of young woman's breasts. As she sat there holding her empty wine glass, my feelings were complex, but dominated by an overwhelming sadness. That in the bosom of an idyllic world of sunshine, water, swimming, and youthful laughter, such a horrific monster could lurk.

We said an awkward farewell, and she rose and left.

I sat there for a few moments, juggling what now seemed to be serious contradictions. She had cast the figure of someone at home in cosmopolitan settings. Her appearance, her behaviour, initially it all looked relaxed and confident. And yet, suddenly she had shown a very different face, one that exuded uncertainty and trepidation, begging me to preserve her anonymity.

What had her life really been like?

All at once it became hard for me to avoid the sense that likely it had not been good, although I found myself hoping, in a fervor that astonished me, that I was wrong. Her new name most likely was not Andrea Barkwell, but I wasn't going to try to check on that in any way.

Her parents, it seemed, had paid dearly. And there were several ways by which that vengeance might have been exacted.

In the end, I found that I was just offering some kind of silent prayer that at least a part of her future would be sunny.

But in my heart, I feared that it would not be so.

South of the Old Yard

The realization came to me quite suddenly that the noise from my neighbourhood was getting on my nerves. And then I wondered about my neighbours. Did it bother them as well? Or were my neighbours the problem?

In the end, I was surprised at just how short the thought process was, one that led me to the conclusion that it was me who didn't fit in. I wanted something quieter, away from the din coming from the speakers in almost all the local pubs. And then I became aware that I would miss some of my neighbours. There were a few like-minded souls around — like-minded, that is, in the sense that they liked what I liked about our neighbourhood, and disliked what I disliked. But I soon realized that their likes were stronger and their dislikes weaker than mine. They were attracted by the idea of living in an 'in' district, whereas my susceptibility to peer pressure seems almost non-existent, and my desire to be part of a group is more specific. For me, the group's characteristics must be well-defined. Just any group is not good enough.

So, I moved.

And the decision on where to move came so easily that it surprised me. Thinking it through, it became clear that I must have had a target area in mind long before I knew that to be the case. My choice of that target area was all due to my father, really. He had been dead some years, but the area was one that had links to what had been his consuming passion.

Trains.

Old trains.

Trains of yore.

And the trigger to all this, for me, had been the local pub in that target area, The Tank Engine.

The day I made my decision to move, I had a sudden awareness that my mood had changed. Ever notice that? Once the thought becomes conscious in your mind, an interest in changing jobs for example, a decision has already been made, somewhere. No going back. You've reached a fork in the road, and you've taken it. Paradigm shift? Phase change? *Fiat lux*?

As the day of my move approached, I was also approached. By my neighbours. By my pub friends. They asked me why. I gave my reasons, or at least some of them. Some of the people across from me just shrugged, as though to say 'He wasn't really one of us anyway.' A few expressed real surprise, asked why more insistently. I told them, and noticed that on almost every one of their faces there was a fleeting expression of something. Wistfulness? Envy? A fear that they themselves might be the ones who were anchorless or rudderless after all? With two of those people I shared an evening of drinks and heart-to-hearts. I promised to keep in touch with them, and I did. We still get together at long intervals.

I'm too young to know the glory days of steam trains, as my father did, from direct experience, but despite that I've become something of an expert on railways — their history and their lore — clearly more knowledgeable than most aficionados. Let me go back to the beginning though.

My move from the central 'swinging' part of the city took me to a marooned old suburb. It had bottomed out at some point and become an abandoned area of light industry, and was undergoing a resurgence, but an intelligently planned resurgence. It was intelligent and planned only because of the constraints that happened to be imposed. These constraints were that land became available in fairly small patches, so there wasn't the possibility for some developer suffering from FCS to lay out tens of acres of housing doomed eventually, but sooner rather than later, to become a slum. And the demand for housing meant that they weren't allowed to buy up land and then just sit on it, waiting to buy up more. No. The biggest patch offered room for sixty houses at most, and the first of those patches came with space for a school, a library, and some local shops. So the place developed 'organically', as they say. There was no land available for mindless serried ranks of massive apartment towers, all made of ticky-tacky and all looking identical. And guess what happened? Communities emerged as well. All by themselves.

What? FCS? Oh, yes. Foreshortened Cranium Syndrome.

But the whole area was a magnet for developers. They salivated over what they saw as a large space that could be a source of massive profit. And they tried to convince everyone that their vision was the real future. My God, did they try!

There were many meetings, where lawyers for the developers attempted every possible try-on. Wheedling. Cajoling. Vigorous fanning of the fear of being 'left behind'. Dire warnings of social isolation. And then the threats.

One meeting I remember in particular. There was a chap there, another developer's lawyer as I recall, in a suit costing I don't know how many thousands of dollars, who almost blinded people in the front row by the glare from his cufflinks. This man had been scrubbed pink in water that flowed, no doubt, from his gold-plated taps.

"But you won't have a mall anywhere nearby!" he wailed.

A cheer went up.

I had to hand it to him. His feints and pirouettes were masterly.

"Who said we wanted a mall?" someone asked, and applause rippled across the room.

"How many people in your company plan to live in the paradise you want to build here?" a woman asked, not quite suppressing a knowing smile.

The lawyer's mouth worked, but nobody heard what he was saying above the catcalls. At several points, I added my applause.

Anyway, my move was an easy one. It was clear almost immediately that leaving the old area and entering the new one were both actions blessed by the gods.

My father was born in Saskatchewan. His father, my grandfather, had a massive wheat farm, more than four sections. And he was an accomplished farmer who became wealthy. There were three sons, but my father made it clear to his two siblings that the farm would be theirs, that he wanted an engineering career.

Blinks of surprise. "What kind of engineering?"

"Hydraulic engineering."

Their looks of disbelief, as related to me by my father, would have been understandable, since the farm was in an area that would make a pancake look mountainous, and the nearest thing recognizable as a hill, let alone a waterfall, was more than fifty kilometres away.

Anyway, my father realized his dream, became a first-rate hydraulic engineer, walked away from the prairies and the wheat without a backward glance. His career took him all across the country, including back to Saskatchewan, where I was born and raised to the age of fifteen.

Our family lived in quite a few different places, and it was the newness of each place that I remember most. Leaving each place was not a particular wrench, and my memories of all those places were pretty much of equal significance.

Except for one. One thing in Saskatchewan.

A Canadian National freight line ran not far north of my grandfather's farm, and from my years there and later visits to see uncles and cousins, one thing stood out.

The trains.

One can still hear the trains today, or at least the engines. There is a distant throaty rumble as five big diesel-electric locomotives haul more than a hundred cars, loaded with wheat. That's about ten thousand tons of wheat. But then there's the sound of the horns on those trains, long, plaintive, minor chords rolling across the wheat fields. And they relate whatever message is already in the ears of the listener. For me it's essence of nostalgia, a yearning for the ineffable, some combination of the powerful emotions that Hardy, Tennyson, and Coleridge packed into their poems.

Well, 'Chacun à sa propre résonance', as they might more accurately have said.

So, my father took away from the Prairies the sound of trains, something that had become embedded deep within him. He never lost that. And I gained it as well from my time there, but also because he passed it on to me. I still listen to the many recordings I have of train whistles and horns. The sounds of current engines made by GM. Of old Armstrong Whitworth engines.

But then there are the real superstars, the steam engines. Hudsons, Niagaras, Challengers. The Flying Scotsman. The Sir Nigel Greeley. The many Garratts.

I listen to them all.

If truth be known, that really was a big reason for my move away from the central 'in' district, to an area that once was home to a large marshalling yard, all gone now except for lines used by the daily streams of commuter trains, and the large modern maintenance sheds. And my pub, The Tank Engine, sits just to the south of those lines, next to what was a classic and attractive local station, now gone.

I got to know the crowd in The Tank Engine gradually. There are those for whom it's just a pub. And some of those people are 'just' drinkers. Others are there because of beer preferences, or for quiet chats, or to relax, perhaps for the odd game of pool. I quickly identified a group of regulars who stood out.

Those regulars were there for, among other things, discussion that ranged higher and wider. They're an eclectic bunch, and we soon fell into a routine that brought us together once a week.

Very quickly we got past the stage where we had a rough idea of each other's backgrounds, what kinds of beer we liked, and something about families. Hobbies and significant experiences came out gradually.

Hiram is a fairly quiet accountant, and I was a bit surprised to learn of his interest in country music. But his story was infectious. He laughed as he unrolled the account of his life as an office factotum adding columns of figures, while the Hurtin' Music of dozens of country singers spooled endlessly in his head. His account of his musical interest was unexpected, but I thought it was just a pleasant yarn. Until I noticed two of the others smiling at Hiram and nodding in a way that went over my head. Then Hiram just rose from his seat, went to the bar, and said something to the barman I couldn't hear. The barman, a massive chap who has a booming laugh and is called Arnold, went through a staff door behind the bar. I looked at the others around our table, and they just looked back at me. Until the music began, that is.

And the music was a very competent set of opening guitar chords, after which Hiram broke into an entirely credible rendition of Hank Snow's classic "I'm Movin' On". I'm not a country music fan in general, but there are some songs that break barriers, and "I'm Movin' On" is one of them. My table companions watched me closely, evidently deriving great enjoyment from my surprise and my immediate engagement.

When Hiram finished, I jumped to my feet and applauded. Around the table, the others applauded as well, I think mostly for Hiram, and maybe a bit for me. I became a full member that night. We drank rather more than we intended, but I think we all drank both well and wisely, and our laughter echoed around the men's room during each of our four visits there.

It was several weeks later when we got to talking about people's hometowns, and someone asked me where I was from originally.

"Saskatchewan?" Simon said in surprise as we settled into our pints.

It had taken me little time to confirm that nobody in our group came from further west than Sudbury.

"Been there", Lester said. "Well, been through there. Didn't stop except for gas and something to eat."

"Too bad", I said. "Even if you watch Corner Gas, you'll miss the three main things that strike everybody who's there for the first time. At least the three things that were typical of my area." Lester looked sheepish, evidently not knowing, or not being able to remember, what the three things were.

"Where's that?" Simon asked. "I mean, your area. Where is it?"

"It's near the village of Kronau, not far from Regina."

"And the three things?" Jim asked, reflecting the fact that they were all becoming impatient with me.

"The black soil, the lack of trees and hills for as far as you can see, and how much sky there is." They were all leaning forward now. Simon was waving me to carry on. So I told them about my boyhood, about prairie hens, and that the whole place wasn't flat, and that I loved going to see the hills and trees that were about an hour's drive away from where my father and I lived on the outskirts of Regina, and from my grandfather's farm.

Their level of interest and eagerness to ask questions gave me a sudden and unexpected burst of pride, and something else. Something I think I hadn't encountered or hadn't been aware of since leaving the Prairies. It was the whole idea of home, and I was aware then of seeing Saskatchewan again as home, for the first time in years.

So, I spent most of that evening doing a travelogue of my home province. I told them a bit about Batoche, Louis Riel, and the Battle of Tourond's Coulee. I told them about the beautiful Qu'Appelle Valley, Big Muddy Badlands, Manitou Springs, the Cypress Hills, and my first love, who came from Lumsden.

It was a memorable evening.

Just before we left, Lester, one of the quieter ones in the group, asked me "What do you remember most?"

"That's easy", I said. "Trains in the distance."

At subsequent meetings, perhaps predictably, we talked about trains.

"Is that why you live here, in this spot?" Lester asked.

"Partly, yes", I said, and I told them about my father, and how, although he had worked in many places, he never forgot his trains. I even played some of the clips of train horns and whistles that I'd loaded onto my tablet.

That really unleashed the questions.

"Have you actually seen some of those engines?" (Simon)

"How many of those engines are still running?" (Jim)

"Shit, Ronnie! You've shown us up for a bunch of city thickies. Do you have any pictures?" (Hiram)

"So", Lester said, filling a short pause, "someplace called The Tank Engine is home away from home for you, I guess."

Before I could answer the questioner, Simon introduced another question.

"What's a tank engine?"

I told them.

And then we got into a long discussion about the design of steam engines, and I surprised myself here on how much I knew and could remember. I don't know how it came up, but there was a suggestion that we meet at the Railway Museum in Toronto.

"Isn't that near the old roundhouse?" someone asked.

I said it was.

"We can kill two birds with one stone. Steamwhistle Brewery is just there."

Well, of course that clinched it.

We made our trip. We found a guide who showed us everything, walked the legs off a couple of our group. Related a lot about old steam engines.

"You're kidding!" someone said.

"Well", I challenged. "What else do you think would make a steam engine chuff?"

"Well, I … I don't know. I guess … I never thought about it!"

"So the steam from the cylinders at the end of the expansion stroke is just vented to the firebox? Why?"

"Why not?" I said. "It's got to go someplace. And by venting it through the firebox the burning coal is fanned."

"Well shit! I'll be damned!"

Several weeks later, back at The Tank Engine, we tied off a lot of factual loose ends from that trip. Our evenings now had become open-ended, free-ranging, and quite strongly companionable. All the rest of them came from Ontario, and all but Lester, who was the one from Sudbury, were very local. But I noticed that we had begun talking more about other places, spots further away.

Looking back, I suppose the idea arose gradually, in stages. But then eventually it was on the table. It was Simon who voiced it.

"A group trip to Saskatchewan?" I said, dumbfounded.

"Well", Simon said, past a smile that seemed to reflect unanimous agreement from them all, "you've got us interested. We think you'd be a natural guide. Fly to Regina. Rent a minivan, maybe even with a driver, and then go on tour. We can tell you this, though, Ronnie. We're going even if you don't go with us."

Looking out the window of the plane, I could see Lake Superior sliding past beneath us. We were going to Saskatchewan, all six of us. And I was going ... where? Home? Yes, I guess that was right. It had been home for me during some formative boyhood years, and I realized over the course of weeks and months, in talking to my now firm friends, that there were things about it that I really did miss, and that I was looking forward to the next two weeks. Very much.

We were about two hours from Regina.

Images from The Tank Engine, and the Railway Museum suddenly came to mind.

And it occurred to me that although we were more than six miles above the ground, and travelling at more than five hundred miles an hour, it was something other than an airplane that actually was taking us there.

It was a train.

Cucumbers on Fire

William's life was good. But that's because he was in charge of it. All this idle chatter about luck, fortune, was just that: idle chatter. People just seemed unable to see opportunities, and when they did they weren't able to turn them to their own advantage. It was a mystery to William, but not one he spent a lot of time on. Just enough to see what was going on — because someone else's missed opportunity could be his to grasp.

His wife, Catherine, was a good person. They got along well. And that was because she recognized his ability to see through things. This was a skill she lacked, and she deferred all that area to him. Sensible. Logical.

Many years ago, in his early teens, William had recognized the value of humour. Humour helped him read people and situations, because something funny often brought to light a side of people that one had to go looking for otherwise. So humour was very convenient, and William realized quite early that he could make people laugh. He wasn't always sure just why they found things funny, but he knew instinctively what to say and what to do that people would find funny. Then he could just read them. Like a book, as they say.

His work was undemanding. That's because he chose an occupation, supermarket storeroom manager, where what he had to manage was mostly inanimate, didn't argue, didn't complain, didn't struggle. Basically, it didn't get in his way. It was all about having a system in place and then taking the time and the care to get it running smoothly. Sure, he had staff. But they were the sort who were happy just to be told what to do. Frictions sometimes arose, but the staff themselves were transparent, and finding solutions was never difficult. Rarely was any arm-twisting needed.

Every morning when he came into the store, William would stamp his time card, usually make some comment like 'Cell Block C now in lockdown', and head to his office in the storeroom area at the back. He always greeted his staff, but just with a pleasant 'hello', never anything effusive, and always in a way that maintained the bland exterior that they understood easily. His biggest problem was the need to deal with the store manager on a daily basis. The store manager was a prick. He always found a reason to question what William was doing or suggesting. It wasn't that any of this was difficult. It's just that the store manager was never right, and dealing with his whining was tedious. But it was something that had to be done, and William couldn't think of an occasion when he had lost an argument, so the situation was at least tolerable. Moreover, William was always able to send the manager away convinced that the right decision had been made, and that he, the manager, was the one who had found the key to every problem. But William knew that the manager was not much more than a puppet on a string. A tiresome puppet. But a puppet.

William had been working for this particular supermarket for almost two years. It would soon be time for a change. He hadn't discussed any of this with Catherine. When the right thing came along, or rather when he had found a way to engineer the right thing, he would tell his wife. She would agree. He was sure of that.

Work went on, for month after unremarkable month. Didn't matter. The world was a flat place anyway. No reason to expect work to be any different. But he did keep an eye on staff changes, particularly new staff coming in. He needed to know what made each person tick. Opportunities, you see. One never knows when or how they will arise. And opportunities, he had noticed, always involved people.

The staff were a mixed bunch. Many of them had low expectations. There was no sense in wondering about their motivations. Situations were everything. Basically, he needed to know who was involved in a given situation, what their role was, and, if it was a situation that was interesting to him, how others involved in it could be made use of. These were always the points to keep clearly in mind, where the answer to any problem or puzzle could be found.

An ongoing irritant and disruption was the fire alarm system. There were too many spurious alarms. This cost the company money, because there was a charge each time the fire department had to turn out and investigate. But Head Office just paid and pretended that this was a cost of doing business. It was disruptive to William's operation, and he had raised it several times with the store manager. But after a discussion which was little more than an exercise in vagueness, the matter was always shelved, put into a holding pattern by a comment something like 'Leave it with me'.

William knew what the problem was. It arose ultimately from linking a modern fire alarm system to an old electrical system. There were incompatibilities in the interface, and on occasion these incompatibilities would cause a spurious fire alarm to sound. He also knew how it could be fixed, but the fix would involve modifying the interface. This was simple in concept, but complex in its details, that complexity involving costs the store management would not fund. So, the false alarms continued, and William entertained everyone, while gaining the odd flash of insight into people or situations, by making jokes.

"Did you know that a really good fart can set off our smoke detectors? Curried eggs work really well."

"Ahh! Another fire alarm! I'll bet the cucumbers have caught fire again. They're going to burn down the store one day."

"Uh-oh! Fire alarm! Hasn't anyone warned Dorothy about singing in the toilet?"

People laughed. There was little else to do. And so things carried on.

Until one day.

That was the day William noticed what might be the precursor to a pattern. Each time there was a spurious fire alarm, a light appeared on the store's security panel. It took William only a few hours to conclude that this meant the security time lock on the store safe had been disabled. This condition lasted only about ten minutes, then reset itself. He made careful notes of what he saw, thought about it in depth, and then just waited. A few weeks later, the same situation recurred. But until he had seen it recur enough times, he just kept notes and withheld judgment. But then the same sequence of events kept appearing, and William became convinced that cause and effect was involved. William spent a long time thinking about it.

He reflected on this as he drove south, in a new car, stopping at utterly unmemorable places.

It had all gone like clockwork. There had been yet another false fire alarm. The security time lock on the store safe was disabled, just as in all the previous events. But William recognized that this time there had been a coincident electrical fault that had affected several of the store's systems. That wider electrical fault had played strongly in William's favour, but he found out about that only later. In fact, the fault had itself caused a real fire — a serious one — only four hours later. By that time, William had already made his move. The stars were aligned that night. He had been working late on the monthly inventory statement and was alone in the store when access to the safe became possible. He had been able to clean it out without leaving any electronic indication of an intrusion, and when the short term fault had cleared, the security lock on the safe was reactivated. He was still around, the dutiful employee, when the fire department arrived, and they quickly concluded that there had been another spurious alarm.

The actual fire, some hours later, had brought the fire department out once more, this time for real. By that time, William was long gone. The subsequent investigation kept the store closed for three days.

As he drove through Montana, William thought briefly about Catherine, then dismissed her from his mind, for the last time. She wouldn't understand. And it would be days before she knew just what had happened. But it didn't matter. She was no longer of any use to him.

The $350,000 William had scooped from the safe was the equivalent of low-hanging fruit in an orchard, far from any possible security and completely free of surveillance. Of course, the store management and the police worked out that William had been responsible somehow, but that had been only after the safe was discovered empty, an event delayed more than three days due to the investigation. Shortly after reaching that concluson, the store management would then learn from the police of William's death. Because they would discover the body. The great care William had taken, along with some expensive help from a very capable internet thief, made his own dental records just a random collection of data from the records of twenty other patients, widely scattered geographically and having ages that spanned more than three decades. William was now Carl, as his complete new set of ID documents would show beyond question, and anyone doing a search would find that Carl was a man having no past whatever.

William never smiled much, but Carl allowed himself a smile now. Miles flew past as he headed south through Montana. His route would be a random zigzag, the location for each change of direction to be decided at the last minute, and also at random times.

Where was he headed? The need not to be specific about this was a luxury. And his smile broadened as he scrolled through scenes from one of his favourite movies, *The Shawshank Redemption*. He hadn't killed anybody, except perhaps his own persona. Well, that wasn't entirely true, but the body had belonged to some vagrant, a body that would be found in a nearby alley, wearing William's clothes, possessing his wallet, but a body battered beyond all recognition and beginning to decompose. The vagrant had had all the right characteristics, but was a person of no worth.

Carl's future life stretched out before him. There would be decades of it. Flat, unoccupied, featureless, and meaningless. Just like the world itself.

Just the way he wanted it.

The Off-Beats

There are four of us, and on every occasion we just can't wait to get together. And for anyone who knew the details, that would seem very odd, because none of us ever has any advance indication of what to expect at our meetings.

A few things are constant. At each gathering, for example, we will talk about a book, a specific book, one that we've agreed to discuss. But even there, the unexpected is the norm. In a recent meeting, we began talking about Richler's book *Solomon Gursky Was Here*,[1] but within just a few minutes we had shunted into a long, detailed, and argumentative consideration of the history of bagels.[2] The sort of arrangement we have works because everybody loves discussion, is well informed, adores uncertainty and indeterminacy, relishes unexpected byways, and will strive to debunk, derail, and demolish any hint of the modern obsession over being certain about everything.[3] And we will not just strive, we will strive mightily, strive until the last dog has been hanging for weeks.

To highlight just one aspect of all this, when Gursky went into our verbal electrofragmentizer[4] and bagels came out, even that

---

[1] Richler was accused of writing the same story over and over again. Not true, obviously, since all his books have different titles.

[2] See *The Bagel: The Surprising History of a Modest Bread*, by Maria Balinska. Nothing tells the full story though, and you really need to eat a few in order to 'know'.

[3] See the book *Doubt: A History*, by Jennifer Michael Hecht, even though there's some question on whether it will contain what you want.

[4] You will be told that an 'electrofragmentizer' has something to do with 'Darkroom 1 2013', a strange video that I'm sure won't interest you. There's no point anyway, because there's really no connection.

discussion was subject to the delights of conversational hijack, because, when spoken, the words bagel and bagle[5] can't be distinguished, both being legitimate. Someone raised the spectre of bugles. Well, then, beagles were not far behind, and then bangles, and inevitably biggles.[6] By the time a full review of William (W. E.) Johns and an equally productive (?) sideways leap into Bartholomew Bandy and Donald Jack[7] had blown themselves out, we were searching the horizon for recognizable headlands. Bogles[8] came to the rescue, but the question in the air immediately was 'Which kind of bogle?' And was Kenneth Williams' usurpation of the word[9]

---

[5] A bagle is something carried by a bishop. Or one of those guys. It's a crook. I've heard it called a crozier as well. I think. No, I mean the thing he carries, it's wood and it's a crook. Well, okay, he might be a crook too, I have no idea. The thing is, if you see one of those guys, carrying one of those things, stay well away from him. If he gets close enough, he'll have the thing around your neck. Then you'll be dragged off to a monastery and the top of your head will be shaved bald.

[6] James Bigglesworth (Biggles) is a fictional character created by Captain W.E. Johns. A short description won't work. There are something like 98 Biggles books.

[7] There are lots of reasons for reading *The Journals of Bartholomew Bandy* by Donald Jack. One of many scenes I recall was his talk at a girls' school. He flew his Sopwith Camel to the school and gave a talk to a group of girls on how he saw the war (First World War), but warmed to his subject a bit too much. He gave an animated description of a dogfight, in which he was surrounded in the sky.

'There were fokkers on the left, there were fokkers on the right...'

The headmistress became concerned.

'Girls, girls', she said. 'A Fokker is a kind of airplane.'

Bandy, still in full cry, responded.

'These weren't Fokkers. They were Messerschmidts.'

[8] A bogle is a scarecrow. Originally a Scottish scarecrow. It might wear a kilt. Not sure. Now that would be scary. Especially in a high wind.

[9] Kenneth Williams did performances as a character he called Rambling Syd Rumpo. Syd had some fairly ambiguous lyrics, and they were given extra juice by the rustic accent Williams gave him, from deep in a county somewhere in southern England. You'll hear people brand his skits as lewd, but keep an open mind. One of these skits was a song entitled "The Song of the Bogle Clencher", the first verse of which is, well, on second thought, maybe you could just look it up.

allowed? And what about the singular in general? A person's name, for instance? Eric Bogle,[10] as an example? Things really went on the rocks when the suggestion of bargles was tabled. There were catcalls. A demand arose for demerit points to be assigned. Bargles was backpedalled to bargle but that was disqualified immediately since the argle[11] part was missing. Thirst and our proximity to good wine got things back on the rails.

I used the word 'everybody' some time back. I mean all four of us. As a group, we go by various names. The Roister Doisters[12] was popular for a time. The Eigenvalues[13] flared to life for a decent interval. Poubelles Amoureuses[14] held favour for a few weeks. Names still come and go, but mostly now it's just Us Guys.

Our most recent evening was serenity itself in comparison. We had decided to tackle something of a potboiler novel, *When Eight Bells Toll* by Alistair MacLean. We all enjoyed it, and not just because the Good Guys won. There were some nice descriptions. The spies and villains, always evil and despotic, were delights. Cheers went up for the Good Guys when they were able to abandon their psychological missionary positions long enough to do some dastardly things. After all, they were only human, missionary stances notwithstanding, and somebody has to strike blows for Truth and Freedom.

---

[10] Born a Scot in 1944, Eric Bogle has lived in Australia since he was twenty-five. He is a singer-songwriter, and if all he had ever written was "The Green Fields of France", his reputation would be justly secure. But he has written many, many more songs.

[11] Argle-bargle means to dispute or wrangle. Bargle, on its own, is a decent-looking word candidate, but it hasn't found a meaning yet.

[12] *Ralph Roister Doister*, by Nicholas Udall, written probably in 1552, might have been the first comic play in English.

[13] Eigenvalues are a special (note the word 'special') set of scalars that occur with a linear system of equations. For those who know what they're doing, eigenvalues pop out, magically, from matrix equations. Sometimes eigenvalues are also called characteristic roots, characteristic values, proper values, latent roots, and maybe even girdling roots, protruding roots, aerial roots...Look! I'm just an engineer.

[14] *Poubelles Amoureuses*. You're on your own with this one I'm afraid. But it sounds good.

What turned out to be the central question of the evening delighted everyone and for a moment it stopped the conversation cold.

"What about clocks?"

Did that mean water clocks? Candle clocks? Incense clocks?[15]

"I was thinking of Leroy Anderson."

At this, the others became truly stopped clocks, but here suddenly was Anderson, one of my heroes, front and centre. Hearing his music marked the beginning of my love of trumpets. But then, across the table from me, Allan's face lit up, and I roared an oath inwardly, since it was clear that someone had got there before me.

Allan raised an index finger, claiming the floor.

"Two of the lines have to do with Professor Einstein being called, and his sad confession that there was nothing he could do."

"Yes!" I exclaimed. "The Syncopated Clock!"

"Well, okay!" came a wine-soaked rumble from a far corner. "This opens lots of possibilities. Like how the passage of four hours came to be known as eight bells. Except for dog watches, of course. And why Anderson settled on a syncopated clock."

"That shouldn't slow us down too long", said Errol. "Surely it's just the general fascination over the impossibility of 'tock-tick'."[16]

"Impossibility?"

"Well, yes. It's a rule, an unbreakable linguistic rule. Anderson just used some sheet music to restate it."

There was some commotion at the gloomy end of the table.

"I ... it was ... why can't I ... Shit! Who stole the tacos?"

"Hey! Good one Jim! Tachos![17] I love it!"

"Unbreakable rule? What the... ?"

"Yeah! It's true. You never hear about the Bad Big Wolf. Nobody talks about a pleasant and green land. To everything there's an order!"

---

[15] Like candle clocks, except they burned sticks of incense.

[16] See *The Elements of Eloquence*, by Mark Forsyth.

[17] Tachos, some people would have you believe, are actual food things. I like to believe that they might be fast (or slow) acting tacos. But in the end, whatever they might be, they'll have something to do with speed, as in tachometer, tachyons, tachycardia...

192 Fool's Cap and Other Stories

"Turn, turn, turn!"[18] someone was heard to mutter.

"Speaking of order", I intoned, "let's cast a wide net. We can think back to Harrison's clocks and the problem of longitude. That was really the difficulty of keeping *accurate* time over a long period. There were no timepieces better than Harrison's[19] for a long time. Sorry. A long while. But then in the twentieth century, it became apparent that there are good reasons for our long-standing puzzlement over time, what it is actually. Dear old Albert showed everyone that we need to be careful about time. And then after mid-century, when time-keeping became very precise, it was a routine exercise to show that Einstein's theory was correct, that a clock sitting on the ground in the back garden behaves differently from one on a night table on the second floor. The clock on the ground runs more slowly."[20]

"What's this got to do with Anderson?" Jim asked, having retrieved the tacos.

"Well, nothing", I said. "Why does it need to have anything to do with Anderson?"

Point scored.

"Why did he write 'The Syncopated Clock'? What was he hoping to achieve?"

"Why did he write 'Bugler's Holiday', or any of quite a few other pieces?" I countered. "I think he had a good tune in mind, then he found some words."

"What's a dog watch?" The question emerged from the conversational mist, as if inspired by the Mary Celeste.

"I've always thought that Anderson was playing a trick with "The Syncopated Clock". People don't think of him as subtle, but

---

[18] Thanks to Ecclesiastes and The Byrds.

[19] John Harrison, born in 1693, was a self-educated clockmaker who built the world's first true chronometer. He was cheated out of the Longitude Prize, but was awarded the Royal Society's Copley Medal. See the book *Longitude* by Dava Sobel.

[20] Clocks just a few feet apart and running at different rates because of that? Too incendiary. They won't let me explain it. But Carlo Rovelli can tell you about it in his book *The Order of Time*.

in the case of that song I think he was. Without saying that the clock was going 'Tock Tick', his words tell you that everyone was baffled. It's like the Bad Big Wolf. It's an unwritten rule. Everybody knows it. But they don't realize they know it until it's been broken in public."

"Not sure what a dog watch is exactly", Errol said, stepping into the fray with thoughtful absent-mindedness. "It was a watch at night, I know that much. And I think it had some connection to the Royal Navy mutiny at Nore[21] in 1797."

"They're over here, Jim", I said, sensing the imminent onset of more taco agitation.

"When was the last time anybody heard 'The Syncopated Clock' played?"

We all looked around at each other.

"Long time..."

"Years..."

"I think it won't come across unless you have a superheterodyne[22] radio..."

"Not a reason. All radios are superhet today..."

"This wine bottle's too heavy to be empty..."

"It isn't empty. The cap's still screwed on..."

"Which scurvy swine stole my panini...?"

"Nobody stole it. It fell into your lap..."

"Pigs don't eat bread, do they...?"

"Of course. Pigs'll eat anything..."

"Time to charge your thunder jugs, you band of rowdies", I barked. "Let's drink to Leroy Anderson, the old clever sod."

---

[21] There were two mutinies that year, one at Spithead and a second, more serious, at Nore. It seems that sailors wanted decent food, drinkable water, to be looked after when they were sick or injured. Yes, indeed. Totally unreasonable. Richard Parker is generally known as the tiger in Yann Martel's book *Life of Pi*. Alas, the real Richard Parker was the chief mutineer at Nore, and was hanged in the same year as the mutiny.

[22] Superheterodyne. Great word. 'Dyne' is a metric unit, so 'superheterodyne' sounds as though it might be a really, *really* straight kind of dyne. Yes, I'm an engineer, but a chemical engineer. Electrical stuff always baffled me.

There were catcalls and a few chuckles. We all stood and raised our glasses.

A chair fell over.

"Shit! I've spilled the tacos!"

Glasses met and the voice of crystal rang out in the room. Wine vanished into four smiling men. By that time, none of us was clear of eye or mind any longer.

A modest eructation was suppressed, with incomplete success.

"Pardon me."

"Not a problem, Sir Toby."

We sat down and clutched at more passing threads of discussion, and the evening continued as, imagining ourselves in full dress, we executed beautiful, if virtual, caracoles well into the wee hours.

At least according to the clocks in that room.

Acknowledgment

I want to thank my editor, Lee Parpart, for excellent comments and suggestions, both specific and general.